DAWN OF THE ENEMY

A Raina Storm Thriller – Book Two

Kim Cresswell

KC Publishing
Ontario, Canada

KC Publishing
London, Ontario Canada

Publisher's Note: This is a work of fiction. Names, characters, places, and incidents are a product of the author's imagination. Locales and public names are sometimes used for atmospheric purposes. Any resemblance to actual people, living or dead, or to businesses, companies, events, institutions, or locales is completely coincidental.

Cover Art © 2018

Ordering Information:
Quantity sales. Special discounts are available on quantity purchases by corporations, associations, and others. For details, contact the publisher at the address above.

Dawn of the Enemy/Kim Cresswell. – 1st edition.
ISBN 978-0-9950578-9-0

For Justin, Carla, Porter, and Peyton

In memory of Mary Beech

Death leaves a heartache no one can heal, love leaves a memory no one can steal.
– From a headstone in Ireland

CHAPTER ONE

Bangkok, Thailand

Raina Storm clutched her daughter's hand, the six-year-old's skin warm against hers, and steered through the mob of shoppers in Yaowarat, Bangkok's two-hundred-year-old Chinatown district. In the distance, bells rang, the elegant donging evoking the gods and keeping the evil forces at bay, or so the locals believed. As they strolled by one of the many street food stalls selling Pad Thai, boat noodles and suckling pig, the savory sweet smell of curry, cardamom and other delicate spices mingled around them.

Jayden pinched her nose. "Phew, Momma. That stinks."

Raina smiled and wondered if her child would ever get used to the cultural differences, let alone the banquet of Thai food she refused to eat. Sweat pooled and trickled down between her shoulder blades, her skin slick with wetness under her army green tank top. She glanced at her watch. It was one in the afternoon, the February heat unbearable, and it would only get worse as the day progressed. Dozens of pumpkin orange and gold-foiled paper lanterns hung above on wires and swayed and rustled in the stifling hot breeze, sounding like crumpled cellophane.

"Momma. Look!" Jayden's big round eyes lit up, and she pointed to a towering pyramid-shaped display of fruit at one of the vendor stalls.

She eyed the apples and bananas, her daughter's favorites. "Finally, we found something *you* will eat."

Jayden pushed her tousled bangs out of her eyes and giggled.

After paying one hundred and sixty baht in coins for fruit for her daughter and dragon fruit for herself, Raina adjusted her black leather shoulder bag, ready to get out of the heat and go home. Jayden's brown hair flopped in the wind as she skipped beside her, humming an unrecognizable song, oblivious to the heat or anything else.

They'd been living in a furnished, air-conditioned two-bedroom condominium for the past three months after leaving the US following the catastrophic attack at the Diablo Canyon Nuclear Plant, the deadliest act of terrorism since 9/11. After the attack, Raina had helped destroy a dirty bomb in Colombia before the same terrorist cell working with the *Sur del Calle* cartel could transport the device into the US and detonate it. Their plan? To take out another nuclear facility. As if one strike wasn't enough. The devastation would last for decades. Luckily, the bad guys had failed the second time around.

She hadn't signed on for the mission, instead was blackmailed into 'lending a hand' if she didn't want to see her daughter taken away and placed in a foster home. It all worked out in the end. The terrorists were dead, and the death toll had included some of the cartel's major players. Another deadly situation defused. She wasn't naive enough to think more attacks weren't coming, but for now, she felt safe in Bangkok, away from the fallout on the west coast of the United States.

She glanced over her shoulder and observed two muscular Asian men dressed in tight fitting black T-shirts and jeans strutting twenty yards behind her, their black hair glistening in the sunlight. It was their body language, the way they moved with purpose and commitment that caught her eye. The hairs on the back of her neck rose. They didn't look like the type of men who wanted to have a friendly chit-chat.

This can't happen now. Not when she was with her daughter.

Raina had seen it before. Too many times. Somehow, her past always found a way to catch up with her. She also knew it would be just a matter of time before others would show up. They always did. Concern swirled inside her. She didn't know who the men were but could only guess they were connected to one of her past assignments with the CIA, or someone else she had angered along the way. She wasn't planning on sticking around to find out. She tightened her grip on Jayden's hand and hastily weaved through the frenzy of shoppers and tourists, determined to lose her newly acquired followers.

"Too fast, Momma."

"I know, baby." Raina stopped and picked Jayden up, balancing the child on her hip before quickening her pace. "We need to hurry so you can have some bananas and juice."

Jayden smiled and wrapped her arms around Raina's neck.

Raina glanced over her shoulder again. The men were still trailing them. She needed to lose them.

As she rushed through the dizzying maze of trinket, jewelry, and fabric vendors thronged with shoppers haggling over prices. Chinese signage in brilliant shades of pink, yellow and red creaked in the wind, the sound unnerving. She made a quick right, leaving the mob of bargain hunters behind, and jogged down a long narrow alley. She threw a final look over her shoulder. The two men closed in on her. The familiar pop of a suppressed 9mm Glock sounded much like a firecracker going off.

The sound startled Jayden, and she began to cry.

She held her daughter tight and ducked. "It's okay. Hang on, sweetie."

A slug whistled past Raina's head and thumped into a stack of broken wooden crates. She veered right and bolted, the soles of her leather sandals pounding the hot pavement.

Another pop. Then another.

She sprinted around a corner and spotted a large metal garbage bin ahead, outside the back door of a restaurant. She picked up her speed, determined to put some distance between her and her attackers.

A half a block later, her legs burned. Raina came to an abrupt stop, placed Jayden on the ground, and pulled her behind the bin. "I need you to stay right here." She lowered her voice, almost to a whisper. "Stay very quiet, and don't move even if you hear something really scary. Okay? Promise?"

Fear, confusion, and tears filled her daughter's eyes. She nodded slowly and crouched, resting her small hands on her knees.

A dog barked. Aggressive car horns honked, the sound coming from the main street.

"Momma will be right back." Raina dropped her shoulder bag next to her daughter then ran back in the direction of her attackers. She flattened her body against one of the buildings and waited.

The men had guts, unloading their weapons in broad daylight, especially in such a busy tourist area surrounded by majestic religious temples. They even had more guts, thinking they could get away with scaring her daughter.

She swiped the sweat from her eyes. This was the last thing she wanted to do in front of Jayden, but there was no other option. She was sick of spending her life always looking over her shoulder because of her past. It was like a large toxic cloud, dictating every decision in her life, and right now, protecting her daughter was first and foremost. Whoever these men were, they needed to be stopped.

Thudding footsteps approached.

She inhaled a deep breath and exhaled. Perspiration dripped from the tip of her pony-tail and slid down her back, chilling her body.

The first man crept past her, his Colt .45 aimed and readied as he headed in the direction where Jayden was hidden. The second man was nowhere in sight.

Raina ran.

Six long strides and her right foot struck the wall first. She sprinted up the side of the brick building, leapt into the air and side-kicked the gun from the man's hand with such impact it broke his arm. The brutal force of the blow slammed him to the ground.

He lay on his side, dazed for a long moment then clutched his fractured and useless appendage.

She grabbed his gun and stood in front of him with the barrel of the weapon trained at his head. Her breath came out in short, forceful rasps. "Who are you?"

The man's features twisted with pain. He clenched his teeth and shook his head.

She could almost read the man's mind by the look of surprise in the back of his eyes as he realized he'd just been taken down by a woman who weighed a hundred and twenty pounds.

Raina jabbed the weapon in his forehead and held it there, a reminder she wasn't playing games. "One last time. Who are you and who sent you?"

He stared at her with fierce dark eyes, as if calculating his next move. A small smile curled the corners of his mouth. He shook his head again.

She pressed the barrel into his skin hard enough to leave an indent. "If you move, you're dead."

Another pop.

A bullet hissed past her ear, too close for comfort.

She jumped out of the line of fire and observed the second man zig-zagging through the alley. He looked like an enforcer, overly ripped, his neck the size of his upper thigh. He stopped and ducked behind a discarded wooden door, the top of his large head visible enough for her to get off a clean shot. Then Raina heard her daughter's gentle sobs. Her eyes instinctively snapped to the bin where Jayden was safely tucked away, out of harm's way. The child was terrified. *Hang on, baby. Just a few more minutes.* Guilt flooded her body and her heart squeezed. This was not a situation she wanted her daughter to witness.

Out of the corner of her eye, she caught movement beside her. The man wasn't going to stay down, apparently determined to fulfill a death wish. She would be more than happy to oblige if it meant keeping her daughter safe.

She whirled and confronted her assailant.

He bounced to his feet and lunged at her.

Her heart rate accelerated. Raw adrenaline shot through her veins, and she fired the weapon.

The bullet penetrated his left eye and bored into his brain, leaving the left side of his skull shattered. His body jerked then fell backwards. What was left of his head bounced like a rubber ball against the ground then finally lopped to one side while his hand lifelessly clung to his weapon.

Raina crouched next to the body and watched Enforcer-guy moving closer, using whatever he could find tossed in the alley to help shield himself.

This time, she wasn't asking questions first.

She stood and scrambled to the corner of the building, the handle of the Colt .45 gripped tight in her hand.

This needed to end as quickly and quietly as possible. She had to get back to Jayden. The longer they were in the alley the more likely someone would stumble upon them and contact the authorities—trouble Raina didn't want or need.

She poked her head around the corner. Sweat stung her eyes and slid down the sides of her face. She blinked.

Enforcer-guy fired.

A round buzzed past and drilled into something behind her with a hollow clunk.

She held her breath and stepped out from the corner with her gun ready.

The man decided to run to the other side of the alley but didn't get far. Her shot to the side of his neck stopped him dead in his tracks. Blood sprayed and showered down around him. He fell in a crumpled pile, his legs splayed crudely out around him as if broken.

Relieved it was over, Raina exhaled and tucked the Colt .45 in the back of the waistband of her shorts and covered it with her tank top. She would have to make a brief stop at the apartment and grab her burner cell phones, their passports, her emergency stash of cash and the gun she'd purchased for twenty-three hundred US dollars on the black market in Khlong Thom, where you could buy anything from fake passports to AK-47 rifles. It was a dangerous move to go to the apartment, but a necessary one. She also didn't have anyone in Bangkok she could trust to look after her daughter. Checking into a hotel, for now, was her only option, at least until she could figure out who was after her.

After quickly searching both bodies and collecting two wallets, Raina ran back to Jayden. As she approached, her daughter's sobs grew louder. The thought of Jayden upset made her feel even worse about what she had been forced to do. She stopped, and her eyes shifted to the ground. A thin stream of blood snaked out from behind the bin.

Raina's heart stopped, and fear froze her limbs. "Jayden!"

CHAPTER TWO

"Where are you, Donahue? It's almost eleven." Hal clutched his cell phone and scanned the sprawling staging area at Nellis Air Force Base filled with executives from the Nuclear Regulatory Commission, FEMA workers, state nuclear power plant operators, state and local officials, as well as over three-hundred volunteers and first responders: police, firefighters, and medical personnel.

"I'm ten minutes out. There was an accident on Las Vegas Boulevard. Traffic's backed up."

The mid-morning sun beat down on his back and made his cotton T-shirt cling to his skin. "They'll be starting soon. It's almost time."

"You worry too much, Decker. It's not as if we haven't done a nuclear disaster preparedness exercise before. And it won't be the last time. I'll be there soon."

He disconnected the call and shoved the phone into his shirt pocket.

Angela was right. This was the second practice run since the terrorist attack at the Diablo Canyon Nuclear Plant three hundred miles away in California.

Months later, the death toll had risen to over twenty-seven hundred with another six hundred were sick with radiation poisoning and expected to die within the next three months—if not sooner. Men, women, and children. The thought sat heavy in his heart and mind.

Although he was no longer active with the Bureau and Angela was ex-military, they had worked together on a few covert operations, including neutralizing a dirty bomb en route to the US.

He and Angela were a new breed of former agents, freelancers. With that came a duty to volunteer for these exercises, especially after 9/11 and Diablo Canyon. He rubbed the back of his neck and noticed his former SAC, Trent Chambers, walking toward him, sporting a navy-blue golf shirt and jeans. His thin face betrayed nothing but arrogance.

"Surprised to see you here, Decker. A bit out of your realm of expertise."

The guy was a hardcore asshole—always had been. Hal was grateful he didn't have to deal with the man on a daily basis anymore. A couple times a year was more than enough.

"Donahue and I were here during the last exercise. Guess you didn't notice."

"I guess not. Where is your sidekick?"

"She'll be here in a few minutes."

Chambers paused and ran his hand through his silver hair. "Good turnout, though. We'll be prepared if anything like Diablo Canyon ever happens here. Let's pray it never does." He nodded to one of the officials ready to begin the exercise. "Thanks for helping out. I've got to run. They're ready to begin." Before he left, he patted Hal on the back. "It's appreciated."

Hal scratched his head, taken back by the man's sudden and unexpected gratitude, especially since he'd made it his life mission to irritate the hell out of most of the FBI agents working under him for the past twenty-five years. He turned and spotted Angela racing toward him, waving. Something wasn't right. It was out of character for the woman to be running unless necessary, let alone flailing her arms around. He went and met her.

"What's wrong?"

"This." She gasped for a breath and handed him the tablet. "You've got to see this."

Hal read the headline:

US Whitewash!

"It's all over the Internet and all the major news stations online. Over five-hundred-thousand views on that article alone, and there are hundreds of them, all saying basically the same thing."

He scrolled farther down the page and couldn't believe his eyes. The sixty-eight- degree weather suddenly felt like a hundred and twenty degrees.

FBI agent Hal Decker along with Angela Donahue, a military specialist, and a former CIA agent only known as Storm, blew up a nuclear dirty bomb in Colombia during a recent secret mission that killed hundreds of women and children. The death toll included the US sanctioned killing of Alejandro Quintero, the head of the Sur del Calle cartel...

When he read there was a thirty-million-dollar bounty on all three of them, he shook his head and clutched the tablet until his fingers turned white. "Where the hell did they get this information? It was a covert mission. There were only eight people on the task force who knew about the operation. Someone paid someone off."

"It's the only thing that makes sense. And where did they get the picture of Raina? It's a bit blurry, but it's her. Someone has been keeping tabs on her. I doubt she'd be impressed to know she's being watched. I can't believe this." Angela's voice filled with panic. "God, it says we killed kids, Hal. Little kids."

He lifted his head and saw the pain in her eyes, the way they glossed over. He understood what she meant. If people believed they had killed kids, it would bring out every fanatic, especially with such a large cash payoff.

"We know it's a lie." He touched Angela's hand and tried to reassure her, even though he knew what he was about to say wasn't true. "It's going to be okay. You better get Chambers. Last I saw him, he was talking with Chief Wilson. We need to find out who leaked the details about the mission and put our lives in jeopardy."

Angela shielded her eyes from the sun's glare and nodded.

While she walked briskly to where Chambers was still chatting with the police chief, Hal's eyes turned back to the article.

There was no mention of Abdul Shakra, the terrorist who'd orchestrated the attack at Diablo Canyon with the cartel's help, or the fact it was

Alejandro Quintero who had helped bring the dirty bomb into his country from Yemen. The posting was propaganda—but propaganda that could get them killed. This wasn't just about him and Angela. His thoughts shifted to Raina and Jayden.

Hal had no way to contact her. All he could do was hope she contacted him. He'd given her his cell number before she'd left the US. Worry gnawed at his gut, and he prayed they were safe.

✳✳✳

Raina dropped to her knees, horrified at the bright red blood running down her child's arm and fingers. A gut-retching stench came from the garbage bin overflowing with decayed meat and fish that had baked in the sweltering sun for days, perhaps weeks.

She wanted to cry but held it in for her daughter's sake. "Oh, baby. I'm so sorry."

Jayden held up her arm. Tears rolled down her cheeks. "Momma. Boo-boo hurts."

"I know, baby." She kissed Jayden's forehead and gave her a hug. "It's going to be okay. Momma will fix your boo-boo."

Bile rose in Raina's throat and threatened to choke her. Bloodstains dotted her daughter's pink sundress. It took all her willpower to stop herself from vomiting. While inhaling through her nose and exhaling through her mouth, she grabbed her shoulder bag and searched for tissues.

After finding a few, she looked at her daughter. "Momma has to put this on your boo-boo. It might hurt a bit."

Jayden scrunched up her face anticipating the

pain.

Raina fought to keep her hands from shaking and held two of the tissues on the wound. After the bleeding had slowed, she gently wiped Jayden's skin so she could take a better look at the injury. Thankfully, the bullet had only grazed her little girl's right shoulder. It was bad enough she'd been hurt in the first place. A shot must have ricocheted in the alley. If her daughter had moved an inch or two to the right, she probably would have been fatally wounded. After witnessing the terror and pain in Jayden's eyes, she was glad she'd killed the two men. Nausea continued to bubble in her stomach, and guilt plagued her thoughts.

She tried not to think about what could have happened and focused on getting Jayden to the main street to catch a taxi before anyone noticed them or the dead men in the alley. As much as she wanted to get to a hotel where she could look after her daughter properly, they'd have to make a quick stop at the condo first. No choice now. A risk. A big one. One she would have to take. She couldn't walk into a hotel with Jayden injured and wearing a bloodied dress. It would raise too many questions and possibly trigger a visit by the authorities.

"Okay, Momma is going to help you up. We need to go home."

"I want bananas."

Raina smiled, amazed by her daughter's resiliency. "Of course, baby. You can have whatever you want." She helped Jayden to her feet then scooped up the dead men's wallets and tossed them into her bag. She needed to know who they were and why they'd tried to kill her. She would have to contact her trusted connection in Bangkok. Maybe he'd heard something on the street.

At the main intersection, compact cars and tuk-tuks, in reverberant shades of yellow and pink, lined both sides of the traffic-congested street. She scanned the busy sidewalks, making sure they weren't going to have a repeat of the earlier events then turned her attention to Jayden's arm. It was still bleeding slightly. The skin around the wound had turned a nasty shade of dark purple.

Once inside the taxi, Raina gave the driver her address and breathed a sigh of relief until she caught a whiff of spices, tobacco smoke, and strong body odor. She rolled down the window. Hot air filled the vehicle, and the breeze only accentuated the unpleasant smell.

"Going home, Momma?"

"Yes. We're going home, baby."

As the driver maneuvered the packed streets of Bangkok, he kept glancing in the rear-view mirror at Jayden's arm and then to her stained dress.

Raina could only imagine what he was thinking. She needed to lie. "She fell."

The bearded young man nodded and remained silent.

Hopefully, he understood and accepted her explanation. If he didn't and decided to call the police, they'd be long gone. Their suitcase was already packed. A safety measure she had put in place years ago. Being prepared, unfortunately, was a way of life when you're always running from the past.

Ten minutes later, they stopped outside her condominium, a cream-colored building with green trim, housing eighty-five units. After paying the driver, Raina climbed out. Her hand instinctively ran along the waistband of her shorts where she'd tucked the Colt .45. She scanned the area, searching for anything that looked out of place. When she didn't observe anything out of the ordinary, she grasped Jayden's hand. She wasn't letting her daughter out of her sight, not for a second.

If the two men who had tried to kill her in the alley knew to find her at the market, there was a good chance whoever had sent them knew where they lived. The building was private and secure, but she wasn't taking any chances. She'd grab what they needed then head to a hotel where she could figure out what to do next.

After cleaning and dressing Jayden's wound and changing her into a clean dress, Raina held her daughter on the open-air terrace and waited for the taxi. She looked down from the sixth floor at the swimming pool and then to the walkways with every horizontal surface planted with luscious green foliage. Not a person in sight. This time she'd told the driver to meet them in fifteen minutes at the back of the building to ensure they weren't being watched. At least the area was shielded by trees, providing some cover, if need be.

"Can we go swimming?"

"Not today, baby. We have to leave in a few minutes and go for another car ride."

Jayden frowned, her eyes heavy.

"You can have some more fruit when we get to the hotel."

Her daughter smiled and rested her head on Raina's shoulder, unable to keep her eyes open any longer.

Four sudden sharp raps at the door made Raina flinch.

Jayden changed positions and remained asleep.

No one ever knocked at her door. She didn't have, or want, any friends and didn't socialize with the tenants, other than to say a quick "hello." Staying under the radar was the number one rule to protect herself and her daughter.

She gently laid Jayden on the white leather couch in the living room then pulled out the gun from the waistband of her shorts. She didn't want to use the weapon unless necessary. She made her way along the perimeter of the room with the gun raised. With her back against the wall next to the door, she strained to listen. Raina didn't hear anything coming from the hallway, other than the quiet hum from the air-conditioning unit. She glanced at her suitcase, and then to the deadbolt she'd installed the day they'd moved in. Her heart thumped as she slid back the lock and slowly opened the door.

An Asian man jumped out in front of her, his bald head huge and round like a bowling ball.

She eyed the government mule-type knife clutched in his hand. Before he had a chance to make his move, Raina curled her hand into a tight fist and pummeled him in the throat with speed and precision, the way she'd been trained.

The lethal hit collapsed the man's windpipe. His eyes bulged, and the knife dropped from his hand. He fell to his knees, gasping, suffocating on each labored breath. Then he slumped forward.

Raina wasn't waiting around to see if he was dead or not. She scooped up her sleeping daughter from the couch and grabbed her shoulder bag and suitcase. It was clear that whoever was after her wasn't going to stop until she was dead.

✳✳✳

Hal looked at Angela, and then at Chambers. "What's the plan?"

This was the first time he'd been back at the three-story FBI field office on West Lake Mead Boulevard in years. From the outside, the hundred-thousand-square-foot building looked like a typical commercial property that might house insurance companies or dentist offices, instead, it was bustling inside with a couple hundred FBI agents and support staff.

"I asked Mike Jacobs to start looking into everyone involved in the terrorism task force. Someone was paid well to leak the details of the operation. Nicolas Artur is working on finding the source of the Internet postings. If we can verify which country they're coming from, it might give us more to go on."

"Artur is a good agent. I've worked with him many times in the past. Smart guy. Ran into him a few weeks ago. I'm guessing the source is straight out of Colombia. There was nothing mentioned about the bomb until now, months later. Nothing in the Colombian media or newspapers. Besides, we still don't have confirmation Alejandro Quintero was killed at the bomb site if he was even there. For all we know, the bastard could still be alive."

"According to the CIA, they still have an agent on the ground in Colombia. At least they had, ten weeks ago. They haven't been able to make contact with him since."

"That's not a good sign," Angela said.

Chambers shook his head. "It's not."

Hal rubbed his chin. "What about Raina Storm? Her death would be quite the prize."

Chambers leaned back in the chair. Deep lines etched his forehead. "She's on her own."

Angela frowned. "She has a *child*! We can't let her go it alone. Not with a price on her head, and not after what she did for us in Colombia. She risked her life to hunt down the terrorist cell and destroy the dirty bomb. Her connections made the mission a success. We owe her. We need to do whatever we can to keep her and her daughter from harm. She certainly didn't help us by choice."

Hal heard the anger in Angela's voice the way her words became more pronounced. His thoughts drifted to Raina and how they'd threatened to put her daughter into the foster care system if she didn't agree to help them. Not a move he was proud of—but at the time, a necessary one to save lives.

"I get where you're coming from, Donahue. I need to worry about keeping you and Decker alive. Besides, Raina isn't known as one of the deadliest operatives because she can't take care of herself. She's an assassin. She'll be fine."

Not with a kid tagging along. Hal wasn't having any part of this. Raina might be the best, but he could guess how difficult it would be to keep her daughter safe, especially under circumstances like these. The last thing he was going to do was leave her high and dry to fend for herself and Jayden.

"Any idea where she might be?" Chambers asked.

Hal glanced at Angela then shook his head and

lied. "No idea."

"I suggest you two lay low until we know what and who you're up against. Stick together. We know how these things work when there's a large bounty involved. Every low-life will be determined to cash in on the payoff."

Hal stared at the tacky landscape painting hanging on the wall behind Chambers's desk. That wasn't going to happen. Laying low and taking the 'sit and wait' approach wasn't his style. It wasn't who he was.

"I've set up a meeting with everyone involved for eight o'clock tomorrow morning. No one is happy about this development, especially the higher-ups. The president is fuming. It doesn't look good during an election year when what was supposed to be a clandestine mission suddenly hits the Internet."

Hal wasn't looking forward to the media frenzy. As of now, anyone who came near them was considered the enemy, hell-bent on killing them.

"Maybe we should go to the safe house until things settle down."

He knew exactly what Angela was doing. They'd be in a safe spot where they could work on finding Raina without Chambers trying to control them. "Good idea."

Chambers nodded. "I'll see you two in the morning. In the meantime, I'll send Mike with you. He can work from there. Watch your backs."

CHAPTER THREE

Twenty-five minutes after instructing the taxi driver to circle the Siam Grand Resort three times to confirm they weren't followed, Raina checked in under the name, Claire Addison, the same name she'd used numerous times. The hotel was one of her favorites, located near the Chao Praya River at the base of the Krung Thon Bridge in the historic Duist district. It was private, expensive and fairly secluded. The last place anyone would look for her.

An attractive butler dressed in a crisp white shirt and black tailored suit ushered them through the lobby decorated in shimmering cream, black Thai silk, and exquisite marble. As they walked to the elevator, the trickling water coming from the circular stone fountain did nothing for her nerves. Neither did the long ferns spidering down from the ceiling. They reminded her of bony tentacles, ready to attack. Her eyes remained fixed on the large open area, looking for anyone who might pose a threat. Luckily, there were only two people sitting on one of the couches: a gray-haired Asian couple who appeared to be in their seventies.

On the second floor, the butler unlocked the door to their Art deco-styled room and handed her the keycard.

Raina laid Jayden on the king-size bed, careful not to wake her, while the butler placed their suitcase on the bench at the foot of the bed.

"Would you like me to unpack for you?" he asked in a thick British accent.

"No. That's fine. Thank you." She handed him a US twenty-dollar bill.

He bowed his head.

Seconds later, she heard the door click shut behind him and she exhaled a sigh of relief. Her daughter was safe. That was all that mattered.

While Jayden continued to sleep, Raina took a cool shower and changed into a pair of black linen shorts and a black tank top. Water dripped from the ends of her long hair and felt good against her bare skin. She dumped the contents of her shoulder bag onto the bed and grabbed the two dead men's wallets.

With Jayden here, there was no way she would be able to visit her contact, Chakan Aawut, head of the Phuket Mafia who ran the corrupt underbelly of the tuk-tuk and taxi drivers in Patong, a beach resort town in southwest Thailand. He was also an expert in forged documents, one of the best she'd had the pleasure to deal with in the past. She would have to courier a note asking him to call her. She didn't want Chakan to know where she was. She didn't know who to trust.

Jayden rolled onto her back and let out a soft sigh.

She looked at her daughter for a long moment and watched the quiet rise of her chest. *Momma loves you.*

Her attention turned back to the men's wallets.

Neither carried much cash. Less than two-hundred-dollars between them. According to their driver's licenses, they were Dusit Chakrii and Klahan Ram. Their names weren't familiar. In a country where counterfeit documents were a thousand times easier to come by than the real thing, the names were probably fake.

Raina searched the ornate wooden desk and found some envelopes and paper. She scribbled a note to Chakan, added the number from her burner phone, and then rang the butler service.

Ten minutes later, there was a soft rap at the door.

She snatched up the Colt .45, slid the weapon into her shorts pocket, and went to answer the door.

"Could you please have this sent by courier?" She handed the butler the envelope. "It's important."

The man smiled. "Yes, of course. Right away." He paused for a moment. "Is there anything else?"

"No. Thanks." She watched him head down the hallway.

She closed the door, hoping she hadn't just made a mistake by trusting the hotel employee. At this point, she didn't have a choice. She needed information from her well-connected contact and sending a letter to his business in Soi Suphaphong was the only way to contact him. If there was any talk on the street about killing her, Chakan Aawut would be one of the first in Bangkok to know. The man was as lethal as his name meant in Thai—able-bodied weapon. Not the type of guy you ever wanted to double-cross, unless you wanted to end up headless at the bottom of a river.

Jayden sat up on the bed and clutched her arm. "It

hurts."

The thought of her child in pain made Raina want to cry. Her inner voice berated her repeatedly for putting her daughter in danger. She felt like the worst mother in the world and had a hard time shaking the thought from her mind.

She unzipped the suitcase and pulled out a small first aid kit. "I know. Momma is going to change the bandage and then you can have some more fruit and animal crackers. Would you like that?"

Jayden nodded, her eyes huge with excitement. She held out her arm while Raina checked and cleaned the wound and put on a fresh bandage. Afterward, she sat quietly on the couch eating an apple and watching an animal show on the television.

Raina smiled. It never took much to make her daughter happy. She grabbed a bottle of juice from the minibar and sat on the edge of the bed, determined to focus on the immediate problem.

Someone wanted her dead.

She took a sip of juice and stared at the dead men's IDs. She had no idea who the men were, other than they were Asian, and their addresses appeared to be local. As far as Raina knew, she didn't have any enemies left in Bangkok. Any adversaries had already been eradicated. She'd made sure of it. Exactly why she had felt safe enough to return.

Sirens wailed in the distance.

She stood and looked out the window at the circular driveway surrounded by lush green trees and foliage. Three white limousines were parked at the front entrance. The area was normally quiet, one of the few locations not drenched with crime in a country heavily plagued with drug lords, gangs and epidemic child prostitution.

As the sirens grew closer and louder, her muscles tensed.

A loud knock on the door made her jump. Raina went and answered it.

"You need to evacuate. There's been a bomb threat."

A bomb threat? Her fingers tightened around the handle of the gun still in her pocket. She stared at the butler, unsure if he was telling the truth or if this was just a ploy to get her out in the open for someone to kill her. She heard voices and commotion in the hallway.

"Please." He begged. "I have a limo waiting for you and your child. The driver will take you somewhere safe. *You* must hurry."

The urgency in his voice was undeniable.

Raina spun around. "Jayden, we need to go right now."

Her daughter pointed to the television. "No. I want to watch the doggies."

She took a couple of calming breaths and quickly slipped Jayden's sandals on, then put on her own. "You can watch some more of the movie in a little while."

The butler already had their suitcase zipped up and ready at the same time as Raina finished throwing the contents from the bed back into her shoulder bag.

In the hallway, panic and fear charged the air, mixed with an unusual organized calm, considering the threat they were facing.

After hurrying down the stairs and rushing through the lobby, the butler flung their suitcase into the trunk of one of the running limos and slammed the lid shut. Raina put Jayden in the passenger seat and buckled her up.

She turned. Her eyes locked with the driver holding open the door. "I'm driving."

He cocked his head. "That's…not allowed."

Raina pulled out the Colt .45 and pointed the weapon at his stomach, careful to keep the gun out of view from Jayden. "It is today."

He half-heartedly threw up his hands and took a few steps back.

A gunshot pierced the air. Hundreds of birds scattered from the surrounding trees.

She ducked. The slug missed her and bored into the driver's thigh. His body jerked, and he fell to the ground.

She kept her head down and crept along the side of the car, praying the shooter wouldn't harm Jayden. She leapt into the driver's seat and slung the seatbelt over her shoulder then slammed the car into drive. She stomped the accelerator, and the engine whined. A hazy cloud of dust kicked up around the vehicle, providing some much-needed cover. As she sped the limo out of the main resort area, a long stream of police and fire vehicles zoomed by in the opposite direction.

A thunderous explosion cracked the air and sent a shockwave vibrating through the vehicle.

Jayden scrunched down in the seat and began to cry.

Raina grabbed her daughter's hand and tried to calm her. "Everything is okay, baby. We're safe. I promise." She glanced in the rear-view mirror.

Raging scarlet-orange flames shot high in the sky and vaporized what was left of the front of the hotel and surrounding vegetation. Bitter, pungent smoke snaked in through the vents of the car, smelling like scorched wood and death. Raina swallowed the hard lump in her throat and kept her eyes on the road, aware that the butler and many of the guests hadn't gotten out in time.

She needed to get Jayden somewhere safe, out of Bangkok. For the first time in her life, Raina realized she needed help.

✳✳✳

After leaving his SUV in the field office parking lot, Hal drove the Bureau issued non-descript black van past the coffee shop on Flamingo Road. His eyes shifted to the side-view mirror and noticed a white satellite news pick-up truck following them. "We've got company. They must have been waiting for us, wanting an exclusive."

Angela glanced over her shoulder. "That didn't take long. We need to ditch them. The last thing we need is the media parked outside the safe house. It sort of gives away our location for any possible…" Her voice trailed off.

Hal heard a slight tremble in her voice. He knew she was scared. Who wouldn't be? It didn't feel good, having a price on your head and never knowing when someone was going to try to kill you.

"We're going to be fine. We have to believe that. I'm guessing out of the three of us, Raina would be the ultimate kill, especially with her past associations." He had no clue exactly what the woman had done in the past, but the intel they gathered before their mission in Colombia pointed to some major assassinations in various countries.

"That doesn't make me feel any better. We're all targets, including that little girl. I'm worried about them. I wish we knew where they were in Bangkok."

"Yeah, me too." His gut twisted, and his thoughts drifted to his last conversation with Raina before she left the US.

"If you ever get in trouble and you need help, call me. I mean that. Angela and I have a lot of contacts and resources..."

He had to believe she would contact him if she needed his assistance. That was all he could do. He slowed the van and turned right onto Harmon Avenue and continued east.

Hal looked in the rear-view mirror and watched the news truck turn the corner, staying a couple hundred yards behind them. "Time to get rid of our friends." He glanced at Angela and smiled. "Hang on tight."

"Definitely, when you're driving." She grinned and grasped the dashboard with both hands.

He stomped the gas pedal.

The tires bit into the road, and the van lurched forward. A block ahead, Hal cranked the steering wheel hard to the left then accelerated and swerved in and out of traffic.

Angela looked in the side mirror. "Looks like you lost them."

He double-checked his mirror and didn't see the truck. At the next street, he turned right and sped back toward Harmon Avenue.

The suburban neighborhood was quiet as usual as

they drove by the two-story safe house. The structure was the most modern and secure facility the FBI had in Nevada, complete with steel plated walls, Plexiglas bulletproof windows, state-of-the-art communication and security systems, interior and exterior motions sensors and cameras, and a metal encased panic room. Once you were inside, you were safe.

He spotted Mike Jacob's cherry-red '69 Camaro parked under a tall sycamore tree across the street.

"We'll go in through the back, just to be safe. Mike knows we're coming. You'll like him. He's a good guy. Known him for a long time. We were in the Marines together." Hal parked at the end of the dead-end street and shut off the engine. He opened the door.

The rat-a-tat-tat sound of an assault rifle filled the air.

"Get out," Hal yelled.

Angela scrambled out of the van and crouched low in front of the door.

The side windows exploded, sending glass showering down around them.

Burst after burst of bullets drilled into the side of the van.

"Where's it coming from?" Angela reached for the Glock 17 from under the seat and tossed the weapon to Hal.

His heart pounded as he inched his way to the back of the vehicle. With his body flat against the fender, he poked his head out for a second, then shrunk back. "The bed of the news truck. One man with an AK-47."

A couple slugs hissed by and lodged into the trunk of a nearby tree with a wood splitting crack.

Sweat spread out across his hairline, and Hal brushed the wetness away. He poked his head out again. Adrenaline spiked, and he squeezed off two rounds.

The man tumbled off the truck, head-first, onto the road, clutching his abdomen.

The driver gunned the engine.

Tires squawked and left a rubbery smelling cloud of smoke and dust in its wake. The news truck sped away like a runaway train, the driver leaving his partner in the middle of the road to die.

Hal turned to Angela.

Pieces of glass in her shiny black hair glittered in the sunlight like diamonds. She looked up at him, her eyes wide with surprise, her skin as white as a bleached sheet. Sticky red blood spread out between her fingers as she pressed her hand over the wound and tried to stop the blood from gushing from her left thigh. "Hal—"

"Shit." She was going into shock. Hal dropped the gun. He hastily unhooked his belt to use as a tourniquet and wrapped the narrow strip of leather around her leg. "This is going to hurt."

She nodded and clenched her teeth.

"You're going to be okay." He tightened the belt around her blood-soaked jeans and yanked hard before securing it. If he didn't, she was going to bleed out. He wasn't going to lose her.

Angela screamed out in pain, and then seconds later, fell unconscious.

Hal's pulse roared in his ears as he loosened the belt and checked the bleeding. When he saw it had slowed, he ripped off his T-shirt, bunched it up, and applied steady pressure to the wound.

Mike was talking to someone on the other side of the van, but Hal couldn't make out what he was saying. He scooped up Angela in his arms and held her close. "Call an ambulance! Donahue's been hit!"

CHAPTER FOUR

After arriving at Suvarnabhumi International Airport, Raina checked herself in the bathroom mirror while Jayden sat on the counter, rubbing her hands together with a ton of soap and giggling at the massive amount of bubbles she had produced. It amazed Raina how much they looked alike; same long, medium-brown hair and green eyes. She hoped they would be invisible in the sea of airport travelers. There was no denying they were mother and daughter.

The bathroom door opened, and four twenty-something Asian women walked in.

Her muscles tensed. She felt naked without a weapon. She'd ditched the limo in the airport parking lot, along with the Colt. 45 and the Colt M1911 pistol she'd bought on the black market in Khlong Thom. She lowered her head and assessed the women out of the corner of her eye, looking for any subtle changes in their body language that could equate as a possible threat.

She hated living like this. Always vigilant.

Always trying to anticipate the next attack.

When nothing stood out, she put on a black baseball cap and pushed her hair behind her ears. Her thoughts wandered back to the hotel.

It didn't make sense. Why would someone go to all the trouble to warn about a bomb threat if their end game was to kill her? A professional wouldn't waste the time or effort. They would have blown up the hotel with her in it. Whoever was after her at the hotel appeared to be an amateur, much different from the attempt in the market alley where the men appeared more experienced. That still didn't tell her who was after her or why they were intent on killing her.

Her cell phone rang. Raina grabbed the phone from her bag and answered the call. She smiled at her daughter trying to blow soap bubbles at her.

"I was surprised to get your note. I didn't know you were in Bangkok."

She recognized Chakan Aawut's husky voice. "I need some information."

"Of course. Anything for you."

She watched the last woman finish washing her hands and waited for her to leave the washroom. She paused for a second, wondering how much information she should reveal to Chakan. "There were two gunmen at the market today determined to take me out."

"Are you injured?"

"No. I'm fine." Raina stared at the bandage on Jayden's arm. Anger brewed in the pit of her stomach. "Have you heard anything on the street?"

"Nothing. Maybe the incident is related to something else."

She had a gut feeling neither of the incidents was

connected to any of her past assignments with the CIA. "The men's names were Dusit Chakrii and Klahan Ram. One of them looked like a gang enforcer."

Long silence filtered through the phone.

"Where are you? I can have one of my men bring you to my business. You'll be safe here."

She'd never had any problems with Chakan in the past, but something didn't feel right—something different in his voice. A distance she couldn't put her finger on. Raina decided to lie. "I'm just outside of Yaowarat. I'll come to you."

She ended the call and swiftly dried Jayden's wrinkly hands. On the way out of the washroom, she tossed the dead men's wallets, IDs, her two extra passports and the cell phone in the garbage pail. Flying back to the US was her only option, especially after speaking with Chakan. The more she thought about it, the more she was convinced he knew a lot more than what he was willing to share.

Clutching her daughter's hand and their suitcase, they walked down the long tubular corridor built with glass and steel. Each time she'd been at the airport, she was in awe of the beauty of the modern architecture that looked like it should belong in a science fiction movie. With over fifty-million travelers passing through the airport each year, Raina had to believe they were safe here. No one would take the chance with so many witnesses.

After making a quick stop at one of the many duty-free shops and purchasing a nylon cord bracelet with blue agate and brass beads for Jayden, they headed down to the main floor ticket counter. As Raina approached the counter, two security guards closed in on either side, their eyes glued to her every move. Her muscles tensed.

One of the guards, with a face like a prune, held up his hand and directed her to stop. The other guard pointed to her suitcase.

Prune-face stared at her intensely and licked his cracked lips. "Come—search your bag," he said, as the other guard ripped the handle of her suitcase out of her hand.

Raina didn't have a choice. It wasn't as if she could make a scene and risk having the police show up. She needed to get out of Bangkok. The sooner the better. She picked up Jayden and followed the two men into a small beige-painted room with a long metal table and two chairs. A camera was mounted above the airport's colorful logo painted on the wall.

The second guard tilted the camera up and away from her then tossed the suitcase on the table and unzipped it. Minutes later, he stuffed everything back inside. "Give me your bag."

She dropped her shoulder bag on the table and set Jayden in the chair beside her.

Prune-face jabbed a stubby finger in her face and smirked. "You shoplift—in store. We see you." His watery eyes drifted to Jayden's bracelet.

It was obvious the men had been following them throughout the airport. Raina watched the other guard dump the contents of her shoulder bag onto the table.

She snatched up the receipt and held it out to him. "I paid for the bracelet. This says so."

Prune-face squawked like a parrot. "Suspicion— shoplifting."

The other guard stared at her wallet and then at her with bloodshot eyes. His expression hardened.

Now she understood what was going on. This was some type of twisted airport shakedown plot.

"He says you shoplifted. The cost is…" He opened the wallet and counted the cash. "Five hundred dollars." He stuffed the bills into his pants pocket, and then chucked her things back into her shoulder bag.

Luckily, she had stashed another five hundred dollars in a secret compartment of her bag that the guard had missed. She couldn't help but wonder how many times the dynamic duo had played this game. Probably hundreds, raking in thousands of dollars a day.

Prune-face laughed and slid the suitcase across the table. "You go now. Bye-bye." He opened the door.

Raina let out a silent sigh of relief. Things could have been worse. The men could have tried to physically search her, detained her for days, or called the authorities. Five hundred dollars was a small price to pay to leave Bangkok. The men should consider themselves lucky they hadn't tried this game on the street. The outcome would have been much different. A few broken bones and the dynamic duo would be begging to pay *her* to leave them alone.

After purchasing tickets to Las Vegas, she sat next to Jayden and waited for their flight to board. With an hour to kill, her daughter was busy sipping a juice box and playing with a package of gummy bears, talking to them in an animated voice before popping each one into her mouth. Raina dug out her last burner phone from her shoulder bag then located the card in her wallet with Hal's phone number. As much as she hated to ask for help, she needed to keep

Jayden safe. Raina punched in the digits and waited for the call to connect. Her gaze roamed the busy area filled with travelers waiting for their flights.

"Decker."

She drew a shaky breath. "I need your help."

"Raina? I'm glad you called. Are you in trouble?"

"Two dead men kind of trouble." She heard her voice break, not wanting to say the next few words because it hurt too much. She swallowed the lump in her throat. "A bullet grazed Jayden's arm."

"Jesus. Is she okay?

Ryan heard the genuine concern in his voice. "She's fine." *Thank God.* "I need to get her out of Bangkok. We're just waiting to board a flight to Las Vegas."

"Good. We need to stay together. Someone leaked the details of our mission in Colombia on the Internet. There's a thirty-million-dollar price on our heads, which probably explains your recent trouble."

Now, it all made sense. Whoever was behind the propaganda and bounty wanted proof of death. The hotel bomb threat was a maneuver to get her out in the open. Blown up body parts weren't good enough to collect the money. They needed a whole body. Thoughts raced through her mind and she didn't like where they were going. The realization hit hard.

Chakan had lied to her. The two men in the alley were his men, members of the Phuket Mafia. It explained the distance in his voice and the way he had tried to evade her questions. She clutched the cell phone tighter. Her daughter had been injured and could have been killed because of his greed. That didn't sit well. She would make sure Chakan paid for his deception.

She gave Hal the details of their flight.

"We'll be there to meet you. Take care of your little girl. You aren't safe—none of us are."

***

Inside University Medical Center, Hal sat in a private second floor waiting room, bent over with his elbows resting on his knees. The room was tension-filled, as cold and sterile as he imagined the operating room was and felt like a jail cell. His body was filled with nervous energy, his stomach jumpy and knotted. His brain couldn't focus. He still couldn't believe Angela had been hit. She didn't look good when the paramedics had loaded her into the ambulance, her skin an eerie shade of gray.

Mike handed him a coffee in a Styrofoam cup and sat on the leather sofa next to him. "She's going to make it."

Hal took the coffee and glanced up at the large wall clock above the surgical suite door. Six-thirty. She'd already been in surgery for almost three hours, and the waiting was killing him. His stomach muscles tightened, and his words came out with forced optimism. "I hope you're right."

The unknown prevailed, in spite of the consoling words from a nurse who poked her head inside the room.

"Chambers said he was on his way. You know Rambo Robot. He has to make an appearance then deal with his favorite sport, the media."

Hal took a sip of the coffee and grinned at the way Mike used Chambers's nickname, which suited the man.

Mike leaned back in the chair. "We got an ID on the shooter. Jason Albright. Ex-military, working at a private security firm in Vegas. He'd also done some 'discreet' work directly with the Colombian government about three years ago. The local cops said they found the news truck dumped on Washington Avenue. It had been reported stolen late this morning. No word on the driver."

He wasn't shocked to learn the shooter had a connection to Colombia. Nothing surprised him anymore. "Has anything turned up on any of the members of the task force? I need to know who leaked the info about the mission because that person is responsible for Angela getting shot." Hal looked up at the clock again and realized less than ten minutes had gone by.

"Nothing yet. Still, have a lot of work to do. We'll figure it out."

Chambers strutted in, wearing his best black suit and groomed to perfection, ready to deal with the media outside the hospital. The guy had always been more worried about the cameras than most of the agents working under him. "Any word on Donahue?"

Hal shook his head. "Not yet. I'm going to need Robson and Russler at the safe house. I got a call from Raina. She and her kid have had some trouble in Bangkok. I'm meeting them at McCarran."

"The FBI isn't a babysitting service."

The muscles in Hal's forearms tightened. *Asshole.* He started to get up. Mike put his hand on his shoulder and stopped him, then stood and stared hard at Chambers.

At six-four, Mike was stocky and as intimidating as hell. He looked more like a hulking bounty hunter or undercover cop than an FBI agent. He still kept his brown hair longer than most agents with the Bureau, at his shoulders, and still wore a silver stud earring in his one ear.

Chambers took a step back and shoved his hands in his pockets. "Fine. I'll send Robson and Russler over to Harmon. Mike, you go with Decker to the airport to pick up Raina and her daughter. I'll have someone else we can trust work on finding out who our task force leak is."

The automatic door to the surgical suite swooshed open.

Hal jumped to his feet the second he saw the doctor through the open waiting room door. "How is she?"

"Stable. She's lost a lot of blood. The bullet severed the femoral artery, but thanks to your quick actions, we were able to stop the bleeding and repair the damage. She has a femur fracture. She'll be in recovery for a few hours, and then we'll transfer her upstairs and monitor her for any infection. She's going to be out of commission for at least eight to ten weeks." The doctor rubbed his forehead, his eyes heavy. "I've got to get back. If anything changes, I'll make sure you're contacted."

Relief flooded his body, and his muscles relaxed. Angela was going to be okay. Hal exhaled, not realizing he'd been holding his breath. "Thanks, Doc." He turned to Chambers. "I want at least two US Marshals outside her room at all times. Guys we can trust. I'm not taking any more chances."

"I'll look after it. I need to go deal with the media. Glad Donahue is okay." Chambers started to walk away then stopped. "Oh, by the way, Vic Serrano and the Whiz Kid are working on finding out who posted the particulars about the mission on the Internet."

Hal was happy to hear two of the best tech guys at the Bureau were working on the problem. But they needed to work faster.

After Chambers left, Mike patted Hal on the back. "Good news about Angela. I guess it's you and me now. Sort of like old times, just under different circumstances."

Hal had to admit this was the first time he had to deal with a price on his own head, and he didn't like it. The last time he had to deal with anything like this was when he and Mike had helped their good friend, Blake Barnett, kill Pablo Sanchez, the former leader of the *Sur del Calle* cartel after the man had kidnapped Blake's fiancée, Whitney Steel. Immediately after killing Sanchez, the cartel had put a price on Blake's head. It wasn't easy then. It wasn't easy now. He looked at Mike. He didn't like putting others at risk, either.

"I'm not happy about putting your life in danger. No idea what we're up against here. If what went down on Harmon is an indication, the grim realization is enemies are everywhere, and we have no idea who or when they're going to strike. And it's looking more and more like the kill order is coming straight out of Colombia. Believe me, that's the last place on earth I want to go after the last mission."

CHAPTER FIVE

At McCarran Airport, Raina stood with Jayden in the baggage claim area and watched as impatient travelers waited to go through the metal detectors while security personnel strutted around, carrying black wooden batons. She thought she noticed a dark silhouette, standing behind one of the columns. Maybe it was her imagination. She was tired from the seventeen-hour flight that included stopovers in Seoul and Vancouver before finally landing in Las Vegas. Jayden had gratefully slept through most of the flight. When she wasn't sleeping, she busied herself by coloring in her favorite book and trying to carry on conversations with other travelers.

Raina grabbed their suitcase from the carousel and noticed Hal before he saw her.

He looked the same as she remembered: six-two and two hundred and thirty pounds of pure muscle. He still had his blond hair trimmed short. Another man she'd never seen before was with him, and that made her nervous. He was attractive, dressed in a loose-fitting navy T-shirt and jeans and looked like an undercover cop. At this point, it was difficult to know who to trust. Money was a powerful motivator, especially when there was a thirty-million-dollars involved. Just when you thought someone was a friend, they secretly became a threat. Like Chakan Aawut.

Jayden ran to Hal the moment she saw him. "I got a boo-boo." She pointed to the bandage on her arm and pouted.

Hal squatted down to her level. "I'm sorry you got hurt, kid. You remember Robson?"

Jayden grinned. "I really like Robyson."

He stood and laughed. "Guess she does remember."

"Believe me there isn't much she forgets." That fact scared Raina. The one thing she wanted her daughter to forget was the incident at the alley. She didn't want her child to end up having nightmares like she had in the past.

"You want to go see him?" Hal asked.

Her daughter nodded, and her eyes brightened.

He glanced at the man beside him. "Raina, this is Mike Jacobs. And this is Jayden."

As if sensing her uneasiness, Hal put his hand on her arm. "Mike's cool. Known him since we were in the Marines together. He still works with the Bureau."

She nodded at Mike then looked at Hal. "It's good to see you again. Where's Angela?"

His blue eyes hardened, and his jaw tightened. "She caught a bullet in the leg. She's okay but out of commission for a while. I'll tell you all about it when we get to the safe house."

Her heart sank at the thought of Angela being shot. "I'm really sorry." She grabbed her daughter's hand, determined to keep her close and safe at any cost. "We need to find who's behind this." Before one of us is dead, she wanted to add but decided not to with Jayden present.

"You're right," Hal said. "I'm not too comfortable hanging out at the airport, considering the circumstances. Too many eyes on us. Let's get out of here."

Mike took Raina's suitcase and shot her a smile.

She picked up Jayden, and they headed to the front of the airport. She couldn't help noticing how some of the travelers stopped what they were doing and stared at her as if they knew her. She lowered her head and quickened her pace.

Outside, the sun had set hours ago, the weather in the low-sixties, the air dry, not like the humid smog-laden air in Bangkok. A gentle breeze ruffled her hair as they walked through the parking lot. Uneasiness ran through her. Raina scanned the expansive well-lit lot, crowded with vehicles, and scrutinized anyone entering or exiting their vehicles, looking for anything sinister. She noticed Hal was doing the same.

Shaking off the lingering feeling they were being watched, she eyed the red Camaro. "Nice ride."

"Thanks. She's my baby. She never lets me down," Mike said as he put their suitcase in the trunk and closed the lid.

Hal tapped the roof of the car with his fingers. "This old girl has gotten us out of a few tough jams over the years. Too many to count."

After Raina got into the back with Jayden and belted her in, Hal climbed into the passenger seat.

Mike started the car, and the engine rumbled. He drove slowly to the end of the parking lot then turned left onto Wayne Newton Boulevard and hit the gas.

"It's loud." Jayden covered her ears.

Raina smiled. "It is, baby."

Probably not the best choice of vehicles when you needed to be invisible. She leaned her head back on the seat and yawned, her eyelids heavy. She unrolled the window and found it hard to fight off the undeniable jet lag setting in, not to mention the fourteen-hour time difference. She thought about Chakan Aawut and his dishonesty. She wished she was still back in Bangkok where she could quickly and efficiently deal with the problem. Whoever had divulged the details of their mission in Colombia on the Internet had a lot to gain, not just financially. For some reason, the whole situation felt personal—some sort of payback.

She watched Jayden stare out the window with her hair blowing in the wind and smiled when the child's expression changed as each car flew by in the opposite direction. She loved her daughter more than anyone would ever know. She felt some relief, knowing Jayden would be secure inside the safe house and in good hands with Agent Robson if Raina had to leave. Her eyes shifted to Hal. Small lines creased the outer corners of his eyes, his jaw tight. He was worried about Angela, and even though she didn't know the woman that well, she hoped Angela would recover quickly.

"We'll be there in fifteen minutes," Mike said as he adjusted the rear-view mirror.

Hal shifted in the seat and looked over his shoulder at her. "I'll call Robson to make sure everything is quiet. We don't want an encore performance of what happened earlier with Angela."

Raina nodded, glad he was taking every

precaution possible to keep them all safe. She also knew from the past that the best laid plans didn't always work out the way they were supposed to, especially when someone wanted you dead.

"Momma, I'm hungry."

"We'll get you something to eat in a few minutes, okay?"

While Hal made the call, she pushed her daughter's bangs out of her eyes and changed the subject, in hopes of keeping Jayden content for a little while longer. The last thing she needed was her daughter cranky. "We're going to go see Robson."

Jayden grinned and clapped her hands together, suddenly more excited to see her friend than worrying about eating.

"Robson said Chambers has the block around the safe house closed up tight as a precaution until we arrive. He has a few trusted locals making it look like they're still investigating the shooting from earlier."

She glanced at Hal. "That should take care of anyone lurking in the neighborhood who shouldn't be there." At least she hoped so.

A bus with tinted windows roared past and finally settled in front of them. Glaring brake lights gleamed off the windshield and choking gassy exhaust filled the inside of the car.

Mike slowed the Camaro.

A loud engine whined from behind.

Nervous tension took over her body. Sensing trouble, she peered out the back window. A two-tone neon green striped motorcycle weaved in and out of traffic, two car lengths behind them.

Not again. Her head swiveled to the front of the car and then to the back.

Hal had his eyes glued to the side mirror. "I don't like this."

Mike looked at him. "Me, neither."

Hal popped the glove compartment and pulled out two Glocks. He handed one to Mike.

The Kawasaki Ninja ZX14-R raced up to the back fender of the Camaro. The driver was dressed in black leather and a matching full-face black helmet. His right hand reached into his jacket pocket.

Raina spotted the glint of the handle of a weapon. "He's got a gun." She slid over in the seat closer to Jayden and put her arm around her.

Mike floored the accelerator.

The back tires squawked. The low grumble of the motor echoed and vibrated throughout the car.

"Take University and circle around," Hal yelled.

Mike cranked the steering wheel and made the sharp right turn at the next street.

The motorcycle accelerated and zig-zagged back and forth a few yards behind the car. The driver fought to steer the bike and get a shot off at the same time.

"We don't want him following us to the safe house. We need to do something."

Hal nodded to Mike then turned to Raina. "Hang on tight to Jayden. We're going to stop him."

She clung to her daughter the best she could. The seatbelt dug into her shoulder, the fabric straining against her body.

"Ready?" Hal yelled over the seat.

"Yes."

Mike slammed the brake.

Raina's heart pounded. She held her daughter and stroked her hair. "It's okay, baby."

The car did a half-circle and came to an abrupt stop in the middle of the lane. Mike killed the engine.

Tires screeched from behind.

Two vehicles skidded to a halt.

Horns blasted.

The driver of the motorcycle was caught off-guard. He had no choice but to ditch the bike down. His head hit the road, bounced, and his body slid about two hundred feet before doing a double roll and smashing into the back tire of the Camaro. The motorcycle spun like a top then rode the pavement hard on its side. Fiberglass cracked and crunched. Broken pieces spewed in the air before the bike slammed against the trunk of a tree.

Hal and Mike exited the car with their guns clutched in their hands.

Raina unsnapped her seatbelt and kissed her daughter's cheek. "It's all over now. We're fine."

This was the second time within twenty-four hours she'd had to comfort her child, convincing her even more that she was the worst mother in the world. Dread pooled in her stomach. The poor child was going to be traumatized for a long time.

She pulled out her cell phone and handed it to Jayden. Distracting her would calm her down. "You can play with this for a few minutes. I'll be right back."

She got out of the car, stopped in mid-stride, and picked up the assailant's SIG-Sauer P226 pistol on the road before anyone noticed. After slipping the gun into her shorts pocket, she looked at the driver's motionless body, his arms and legs twisted in impossible angles.

Hal removed the driver's helmet and checked the

man's pulse. His jaw tensed, and he shook his head.

Blood dribbled at the corners of the driver's mouth and down his chin, his eyes wide and glassed over, the horror of sudden death etched forever in his features.

She breathed an inner sigh of satisfaction that the latest adversary was out of the picture and no longer a threat to her and Jayden, or Hal and Mike.

Traffic in the opposite direction had slowed to a crawl. Curious travelers stared, trying to catch a glimpse of what was going on.

Mike spoke up. "I know him. That's Nick Davis. Rumor has it he's a paid assassin. Former CIA. I met him during an undercover op a few years ago. I heard the guy went underground a while back. I guess thirty million dollars is a damn good reason to come up for some fresh air." He handed Hal the car keys. "I'll wait for the local cops to show up while you take Raina and Jayden to the safe house. It's too risky out here for any of you."

Hal agreed. He put his hand on Raina's shoulder. "Let's go. It looks like evading enemies just became a full-time job."

***

Hal drove the Camaro into the two-car garage of the safe house and shut off the engine. He got out of the car and hit the garage door button on the wall. A helicopter flew overhead in the distance. Chambers must have sent one as a precaution to make sure the area was completely locked down. The heavy reinforced steel door grinded closed, locking them in and keeping any threats out.

Jayden cried out with glee. "Momma, Robyson."

Raina unbelted her daughter, and the little girl clumsily raced out of the car and ran to Agent Robson.

Robson picked her up and grinned. "Hey, Jayden. Looks like you and I have a play date again."

The kid gave him a big hug.

Hal had never seen a kid take such a liking to an agent before, not like Jayden did with Robson. Definitely, a good thing, since he knew they'd need the child occupied as much as possible, so they could figure out who put a price on their heads and deal with the problem.

Raina's green eyes flashed, and she smiled at Robson. "She's really happy to see you. Thanks for doing this again. I feel bad you have to look after her. I know it's not part of your job description."

Robson put Jayden down on the ground, and she grasped his hand. "It's not a problem at all. She reminds me of my own daughters. Maybe one day she can meet my twins, Ashley and Emma. Their birthdays are coming up. They're a year older and just as full of spunk. They keep me and my wife on my toes."

"I'm sure they do. That would be great. Maybe when things quiet down."

Hal hoped things would quiet down, and soon. He stared at Raina. He still had a hard time believing the woman was as deadly as she was, but he'd seen her in action. He couldn't imagine what it was like for her. Always on the run. Always watching your back. It made it difficult to have a normal life with a child. No white picket fences or happily-ever-after endings. At thirty-six, it wasn't a life he wanted, if he ever had children of his own, and he couldn't see that happening in the near future.

"Where's Russler?" Hal asked.

"Inside. He's on the phone with Chambers."

Hal's heart skipped a beat. "Angela? Is she—"

"Don't worry. She's doing okay. She's still pretty groggy. She's been asking for you."

Hal knew he couldn't risk visiting her at the hospital. He didn't want her to become more of a target. He'd already almost lost her. As much as he wanted to see her, he would have to settle with calling her.

While Robson and Raina took Jayden into the living room, Hal found Russler leaning against the counter in the open-concept kitchen. He ended his call and put down his cell phone.

"Chambers said you had some more trouble."

Hal rubbed the back of his neck, the stress of the day finally settling deep in his muscles. "Yeah, a little too much excitement for one day. Mike's looking after things at the scene. He'll be here when he's done. Keep an eye out for him."

"Will do. The fridge is stocked. If you guys want anything else, let me know. I'll do another shopping run tonight. Chambers told me to let you know not to worry about the meeting in the morning. He'll go ahead without you and Mike. Said he'd let you know if anything earth shattering comes out of it." Russler snatched his cell phone off the granite counter. "There's leftover Chinese in the fridge." He scratched his head. "Well, I need to get to work. Chambers has me running background on the task force members. I'll be in the den if you need anything."

"Thanks, man. Let me know if you discover

anything."

After he left, Hal opened the fridge and grabbed a can of beer then sat at the round glass table. Jayden laughed in the other room. It was nice to hear her happy and content.

He was hungry and tired and still worried about Angela. Even though they had dated briefly and decided they functioned better as friends, he still cared deeply for her. The freelance thing was a tough gig. Hard to have a relationship with anyone, since most of the time you were dodging bullets and taking down bad guys. He looked up and saw Raina standing in the doorway. She really was a beautiful woman in an exotic way.

"Russler said to give you this." She handed him the laptop.

"Thanks." He held up his beer. "Help yourself. There's also leftover Chinese food in the fridge."

She pulled out a chair and sat. "Maybe in a little bit. I still have to feed Jayden, but right now she's having too much fun with Robson. I don't want to interrupt them after everything that's happened."

"Don't blame you. It's good for her to have some fun after everything that's gone down." Hal powered up the laptop. "I'm glad she's enjoying herself. It's been a tough day for everyone. Here. Take a look at this." He spun the laptop around for her to see the screen.

She squared her shoulders, and her eyes narrowed. "That's a photo of me was taken right after I arrived in Bangkok. I was looking at apartments with Jayden."

He took a sip of his beer. "Looks like someone has been watching you since you left the US. Any ideas who?"

She hesitated for a moment. "I'm pretty sure an old associate of mine. Chakan Aawut. He runs the Phuket Mafia in Patong."

He heard the sternness in her voice. She was angry. He imagined her friend's betrayal would cost him his life.

"He tried to have me killed at the market in Yaowarat. That's where Jayden was hurt, and then again at a hotel where we were staying."

"Sounds like your associate is looking to collect the bounty money."

She nodded and continued to read the online article. "It's odd that whoever is behind this wants a proof of death picture posted in a classified ad, along with their anonymous email address so they can collect the money. Pros don't work like that. An ad, yes. But usually a post office box is rented, or something like that, and then an encrypted classified ad is placed with instructions."

"We have an agent at the Bureau who was on the task force working on figuring out who and what country the info was posted from. I believe the kill order is coming out of Colombia. It makes sense."

"I agree. Let me try something." She started tapping the keyboard.

Hal leaned back in the chair and waited and watched her work. He had no idea she was a computer crackerjack. The woman was a full package deal.

"Savushkina Street, St. Petersburg, Russia."

He sat up straight, amazed she figured out the mystery before two of the Bureau's crack hotshots. "Shit. Are you kidding me? The Agency?" Hal recalled how the Russian troll-farm known as the Internet Research Agency had been responsible for the Columbian Chemicals hoax spreading terror in St. Mary Parish, Louisiana, and then months later, reported fake Ebola cases in the US, causing some minor media panic.

"It looks that way. But what does the Agency have to do with what we did in Colombia? What's the connection, other than the obvious, supplying arms, especially AK-style assault rifles and machine guns?"

"The Russian mob has been trading arms for Colombian cocaine for decades. There has to be a link between the higher-ups in the *Sur del Calle* cartel and the Russian military or government."

Robson poked his head in the door. "Sorry to interrupt. I just wanted to let you know Jayden feel asleep. I put her to bed for you in the master bedroom."

Raina smiled. "Thank you so much. She had to be exhausted. It's been a very long day. I guess she'll have to wait until morning to have something to eat."

Hal took another drink of his beer. "Hey. Tell Russler to check all the task force members for any connection to Colombia and Russia. Recent trips, family, friends, and associates."

Robson nodded. "I'll let him know." Then he headed down the hallway toward the den.

Her brow furrowed. "How are we going to stop this, Hal? We can't all be on the run for the rest of our lives. It's bad enough Jayden and I are. It needs to stop."

It was clear the mother in her was talking. She'd do anything to protect her kid. Who could blame her?

"We need to find out who gave the kill order.

That's the key. Without knowing, we can't come up with a plan. Let's hope like hell we don't have to take a trip to Russia. Not sure which would be worse at this point. Going back to Colombia or heading to Russia."

"I still have a few connections in Russia, if I can trust them. I'm going to need a few things. It's time to change my appearance, and you should as well since our photos are everywhere."

She was right. Altering their appearances would probably help save their lives. His thoughts drifted to Angela. He hoped she was safe and recovering. He couldn't wait to talk to her.

"Okay. Make a list of what you need and give it to Russler. He'll do a shopping run later tonight." He finished the last of his beer and set the empty can on the counter behind him. "Maybe Alejandro Quintero wasn't at the house when we blew up the dirty bomb. Maybe he's alive. That would explain the kill order. Hell, we don't even know for sure if Abdul Shakra and the rest of the terrorist cell was killed in the blast that day. We assumed they were, based on the intel we had at the time."

Raina stared at the laptop screen then at Hal. "We need confirmation if Quintero is dead or alive. Is there any way we can get that?"

"Not unless the CIA agent on the ground pops up. He's missing. He might have been forced to go underground after our mission or—"

"He's dead." She was quiet for a long moment and stared at the stainless-steel fridge. "Serigo Alfaro won't be any help. He's no longer in Panama. He moved his family to Brazil. Last time I talked to him, he was staying away from the gangs and out of trouble."

"That's good." Hal remembered her contact Serigo. He was a rodent-looking man who had helped them in Colombia. Without his assistance, they would have never been able to get to the location of the dirty bomb and destroy it.

Raina yawned, her eyes bloodshot. She was fading quickly, exhausted from the long flight and the events of the day. The stress of having Jayden injured had probably sucked most of the energy out of her. "How about you try to get some rest, and we'll work on a plan in the morning? Either way, it looks like we're going to have to head to Russia and find out who's behind the kill order. Not a trip I'm looking forward to. I have no clue how we're going to pull this off."

After she left the kitchen, Hal pulled his cell phone from the pocket of his T-shirt and dialed University Medical Center to check up on Angela.

Four rings later, he heard Angela's groggy voice, and all the tension in his body vanished. "Hello."

"How are you doing?"

"I want a cigarette."

Hal laughed. "Guess you're feeling a bit better."

"Not at all. They have me drugged up pretty good. What have I missed?"

"Not much. The locals are still looking for the driver of the news truck. You just worry about recovering. Raina, Mike and I will deal with any threats." He wasn't going to tell her about the Agency or Russia because it would make her worry when she needed to concentrate on her health.

"Raina's there? Did something happen?"

"Yeah. Will fill you in some other time. You need

to get some rest."

"I wish…I could see you," Angela said.

"Yeah, me too. It's not safe. I won't put your life in danger by visiting."

There was an elongated span of silence on the other end before she spoke again.

"Hal?"

"Yeah."

"Thanks for saving my life. I'm glad you were there with me. Stay safe. I don't want anything to happen to you."

CHAPTER SIX

Raina jarred awake and sat upright. Her heart was thumping so hard she thought her chest would explode. Morning sunlight blinded her, coming from the partially open curtains. She squinted and forced herself to slow her racing heart. She glanced at the empty space beside her in the bed and heard laughing coming from the front of the house.

It was just a dream. A bad dream. Her daughter was alive. She breathed a sigh of relief. Jayden was fine.

It was only eight o'clock, and she wished she could have slept longer. She climbed out of bed and saw the shopping bag of items she'd requested sitting on the dresser. She dug through the bag and pulled out the box of hair dye. The color was named Dead Red Valentine. She shook her head. Someone had a demented sense of humor.

An hour later, her long brown hair was gone, chopped in a shorter chic style two inches above her shoulders and was now a vibrant shade of dark cherry red that brought out the green in her eyes. She threw on a pair of khaki shorts, black tank top and a pair of black boots with a half-inch heel. She checked the dresser mirror and barely recognized herself with her new look, which was exactly what she needed. She'd just upped her odds of staying alive. When she walked into the kitchen, Mike and Hal were sitting at the table.

Their eyes widened, and they spoke in unison. "Wow."

Raina smiled and poured herself a cup of coffee. "I guess the new look works."

Mike nodded. "Definitely. I wouldn't know it was you if I passed you on the street."

Hal leaned back in the chair and stared at her. "You look completely different. I'll deal with my makeover in a little while."

Mike laughed. "I can't wait to see that."

"Funny, guy. You're lucky you don't have to do anything. Oh, Jayden has been fed. She ate two pieces of toast with peanut butter, a banana and two glasses of milk. She's in the living room with Russler, playing Fish."

She pulled out a chair and sat, still not completely awake. She cupped her mug of coffee with both hands. "Thanks for helping out. It's helped Jayden adjust after what she witnessed yesterday and what had happed at the market. At least she didn't have any nightmares last night."

"That's good. She's a resilient kid. She's going to be fine. I brought Mike up to speed on what we learned last night. We've come up with a partial plan. The first thing that needs to happen is we need to fake our deaths, a car accident or something. That will buy us some time and, hopefully, stop any attacks so we can leave the country. We'll make sure the accident is distributed to all the media outlets and online."

Mike leaned forward and rested his elbows on the table. "I spoke with Chambers first thing this morning. Once Hal changes his appearance, I'll email the new photos to him for your passports. He's working on the entry visas with the Embassy in Moscow. We should have them by mid-afternoon. He wants us on a flight to Russia tonight."

Raina's heart fluttered. She didn't want to leave Jayden so soon. A mixture of fear and sadness took over. Dread filled her body. She felt the same way the last time when they'd left for Colombia. She didn't want to leave her daughter. Not again…

Hal got up and poured another cup of coffee, emptying the pot. "In the meantime, Raina, I need you to connect with your Russian contact. We'll need a safe place to stay, preferably in St. Petersburg so we don't have to travel. The less in public the better. We'll also need weapons, possibly some explosives, and whatever else you think can use."

She took a drink of her coffee and set the cup down. "Weapons won't be a problem. Vladimir Sokolov is an arms dealer. He's been supplying weapons to Colombia for decades, mainly to FARC to use against the US."

The biggest challenge would be whether she could trust the man. She thought she could trust Chakan Aawut, and that didn't work out as planned.

Small feet thudded down the hallway.

"Momma!"

Her heart warmed. "Good morning, baby." Raina pushed out her chair, picked up her daughter, and hugged her, holding her a little longer than usual after everything that had happened.

Jayden stared at her hair. She raised an eyebrow. "Very pretty hair. I love it."

"Thank you. Not as pretty as yours, though. Yours is beautiful."

She kissed her daughter on the cheek, and then put her down.

Jayden blew Hal and Mike a kiss then she took off skipping down the hallway.

Raina had no idea how such little feet could make so much noise, but they did.

"What's our plan, once we're in St. Petersburg?" Mike asked. "We can't just walk into the Agency and shut it down."

He made a good point. "I'll work on gathering intel through my contact." Raina knew Vladimir was greedy and always liked extra money to spend on Russian vodka and women. "His network is a good source for information, but I'll need some cash."

Hal grabbed a notepad and a pen off the top of the microwave. "How much?"

"Twenty-five thousand. We'll divide the cash between the three of us, so it's not questioned. Otherwise, we'll have to declare it."

He scribbled the amount down. "Good thinking. We don't want any problems with Russian Customs and Border Control. Okay, if we need more cash, we'll have Chambers transfer some through Western Union. This needs to go as smoothly as possible."

Mike rubbed his hands together. "Hopefully your contact will be able to get us the name of whoever put out the kill order. Then we'll figure out what to do about the Agency. Unfortunately, we're going to have to do this one step at a time until we know who we're dealing with."

Hal shook his head then stood. "I agree. Well, let's get some breakfast then get to work. I need to call Angela and let her know what's going on, so she doesn't think I'm really dead when the news hits."

✳✳✳

Later that afternoon, Hal handed a manila envelope to Raina. "Your new passport and cash. Mike will have the flight confirmation in a few minutes."

"Thanks." She opened the envelope and dumped the contents on the bed. "I like your new hair color. Makes you look tougher looking, biker-style."

He ran his hand through his newly dyed hair. He wasn't too keen on the dark brown almost black shade, a stark change from his usual blond hair. "It'll do. As long as I look different from the pictures that were posted online that's all that matters."

Raina flipped open the passport. "Fiona Jenson. Who are you?"

"Jake Thomas."

She stuffed the cash into her wallet. "The name suits your new hair color."

Hal grinned. "The news of our deaths should be hitting all the major news outlets and online in thirty minutes."

He had to admit it felt weird having to fake his own death. There was something sad and morbid about it. But he was glad he called Angela to let her know. He just didn't tell her about going to Russia. No need to worry her.

Raina stood and shoved her hands in her shorts pockets. "I spoke with Vladimir. He has an apartment in St. Petersburg we can use. He said he'd work on the other things we need and to contact him when we arrive."

"Do you trust him?"

She hesitated for a moment. "After everything that's happened, I'm not sure. I'll have to wait until I see him to get a better read. Nothing stood out during our conversation."

"Let's hope he isn't going to cause us any problems. That's the last thing we—"

"We might have a problem. You need to see this," Mike said, his voice filled with concern.

Hal and Raina followed him down the hallway to the den.

Russler was sitting at the desk in front of the bank of flat-screen monitors and pointed to the screen on the right that showed the area outside, next to the driveway. "It might be nothing or it could be something. Might just be a coincidence."

Hal stared at the screen and watched as a moving truck parked in front of the house. The driver got out and looked up and down the street then lit a cigarette. Minutes later, a car pulled up and picked up the man. The driver could have parked the truck anywhere along the empty street, but he chose in front of the safe house. One thing he knew from experience—coincidences never happened when someone wanted you dead.

Panic built in his chest. "Mike, tell Robson to get Jayden to the panic room. Raina, you go with them."

Mike turned and run out the door.

Raina started to follow Mike, then stopped. "What about you guys?"

Beads of sweat broke out along his hairline. "Just

go. You and Jayden will be safe in the basement. We'll be fine."

He knew the structure could withstand a blast, thanks to the reinforced steel frame, but it would depend on how large an explosion. He wasn't taking any chances.

After she left, he looked at Russler. "Call Chambers and tell him to get a bomb squad out here pronto. I don't like this."

While Russler made the call, Mike rushed back into the room gasping for a breath. "They're secure in the panic room."

"Good. Stay away from the windows."

"If it is a bomb, how did they know we're here?"

"I'm guessing from the same person who exposed the details of our mission online. Our task force leak."

"Which also means whoever is the leak is probably aware of the fake media reports about to come out." Mike glanced at his watch. "In less than twenty minutes."

Hal frowned.

"Bomb squad is on the way," Russler said, as he set his cell phone down on the desk.

Hal wiped the sweat from his forehead. "We're going to have to sit tight until they arrive."

Alarms went off. The shrill sound blared throughout the house.

"Where's that coming from?"

Russler hopped out of the chair and checked the security panel on the wall. "The backyard motions sensors were tripped."

Hal's muscles tensed. He scanned each of the monitors. "I don't see anyone."

"There." Mike pointed to four men dressed in

black, wearing balaclavas, climbing over the fence and walking toward the back of the house. "They've got assault rifles and backpacks."

They had come prepared. Hal looked at Mike, who appeared just as confused as he was. "There's no way they can get into the house—unless—shit. Mike, they have the security codes."

"I'll get the guns." Mike ran down the hallway to the storage closet.

One by one, the monitors went black.

"They cut the power." Russler's fingers rapidly pounded the keyboard. "We still have satellite communications."

Whoever the men were, they knew what they were doing, probably fed information from the task force leak.

Hal heard the backup generator kicked on. Monitors flickered then burst to life. "They'll be at the back door in about three minutes."

Mike tossed Hal a matte black Beretta 1301 Tactical 12 GA. shotgun and passed a G36 assault rifle to Russler then pulled out a Glock 17 from the back waistband of his jeans. The three men hurried down the hallway to the back of the house.

Hal pointed at Mike and then to the kitchen.

Nodding, Mike rounded the corner and gave a thumbs-up when he was in position.

Russler pressed his back flat against the living room wall and poked his head out, his assault rifle directed at the back entrance.

Sirens howled in the distance.

Hal's heart pounded.

The back door clicked.

He raised the shotgun to shoulder level.

The door inched open slowly. A black covered arm quickly appeared then disappeared.

A flash grenade rolled across the floor toward the kitchen and rattled on the hardwood floor.

"Flashbang!" Hal closed his eyes just before the blinding flash of light.

An ear-splitting bang shook his body. He stumbled as if he was drunk, disoriented, his ears ringing. His head felt as if he'd been smacked with a chunk of cement.

"Are you okay?" Mike yelled.

His voice sounded like he was talking into a tin can filled with water. "Yeah." Hal fought his way through the head fog, squinting, and trying to focus on the black figure stepping through the open door. His hands shook. He aimed and fired.

The black figure crashed to his knees and slumped forward.

A second attacker appeared in the doorway.

Hal fired and missed.

Gunfire erupted around him, coming from Mike and Russler.

Stray bullets hammered into the walls and sent a storm of dust, paint chips, and chunks of drywall into the air.

Hal dropped to his stomach and glanced over his shoulder.

Raina stood ten feet behind him and to his right with her feet slightly apart, two-handing a SIG Sauer P226 pistol.

She fired.

The second attacker toppled like a tree when her shot caught him in the middle of the forehead.

The third man rushed inside and leapt over the

bodies of his dead crew members.

She stopped him before he knew what hit him with a shot to both knees, forcing him off his feet, his bones shattering.

Sirens grew closer and sounded as if they were coming from the front driveway.

The last man outside panicked and turned. He took off running toward the back fence.

Hal pounced to his feet, his mind still fuzzy from the grenade, and sprinted past the man with his knees blown out. As he went by, he gave the attacker a whack in the side of the head with the butt of the shotgun to make sure he wasn't going to be a further threat. By the time he made it out the door, running-man had already scaled the wooden fence and was out of sight.

Hal stopped and bent to catch his breath. He heard Chambers's voice behind him.

"What the hell just happened?"

He turned and looked at the man. "One of your task force members gave four assholes the security codes for the safe house. There are two dead and one injured man inside. One of them got away. Everyone else is fine."

Chambers puffed out his chest and shook his head. "That's impossible. The codes are changed every forty-eight hours and encrypted on my computer. No one else has that information. Just me and you guys are notified of any changes."

"Then someone hacked your system and got them. How else could they access the door?"

Chambers stared at him for a long moment then changed the subject. "The bomb squad said the moving truck is clear. Nothing but a few empty boxes and moving blankets. It appears the truck was a diversion to keep you guys busy while the men entered through the back yard."

Hal was happy there wasn't a bomb but worry worked through him. How much did the task force leak know about what they were doing? Did the leak know they were going to Russia?"

"Who have you told about the Agency and Russia?"

"Not a soul. No one is even aware the news of your and Raina's death is fake. I took care of it personally."

"Someone is watching or listening to you."

"Christ." His eyes widened with surprise. "It doesn't make sense. None of it does. I'll have the tech guys sweep my office and my home for bugs."

Hal stared at the back of the house. "In the meantime, as far as anyone is concerned, Raina and I are dead and buried." He gripped the shotgun in one hand and started to walk away. "I'm going in to clean up the mess and see if I can learn anything from the injured guy inside. Then we need to get packed and on that flight to St. Petersburg to stop this before Raina and I really are dead."

CHAPTER SEVEN

St. Petersburg, Russia

After a seventeen-hour flight with stopovers in New York and Helsinki, Raina was happy when they finally landed at Pulkovo International Airport in St. Petersburg. Saying goodbye to Jayden hadn't been easy, it never was, but this time was more difficult knowing the safe house had been compromised.

Even though Hal had tried to reassure her that her daughter was safe, worry plagued her mind. He'd gone as far as having Mike stay behind with Robson and Russler and personally re-set the entry security codes himself to guarantee no unwanted guests could enter the house. Nervousness coursed through her body and made her muscles tense. She didn't like being so far away where she couldn't protect her daughter. She told herself Jayden was safe over and over and forced herself to relax.

With her passport in hand, she followed Hal out of the plane and to the second-floor passport control area. She noticed how unusually quiet he had been during the flights, probably trying to digest what had happened at the safe house. Before they had left the safe house, he'd tried to get some information from the man she'd shot, but the guy wasn't talking, nor was he carrying any ID. An unknown, determined to kill her and Hal so he could collect part of the thirty million dollars.

While they waited in line, Raina watched the dozens of travelers hustle and bustle about in the tourist center across from them. She couldn't help but notice how everyone seemed to always be in a hurry and never really noticed their surroundings. Not her. She noted everything, no matter how small the detail. She had no choice. That was what her life had become.

Once their passports were stamped and returned at one of over one hundred passport control desks, they were instructed to take the escalator or elevator to the ground floor baggage claim area.

After collecting their luggage, she spotted the red and green signs marked Customs. She glanced at Hal. "Make sure you have your luggage tickets handy in case they want to check the tags on your bags. I had a problem in the past. Believe me, we don't want to end up detained."

"Definitely not. I think we've had enough excitement the past few days."

Since they were carrying less than ten thousand dollars each, they were able to breeze through the nothing-to-declare green line. Raina breathed a sigh of relief the moment they left customs. At least this time she wasn't stopped by security and scammed out of money like in Bangkok.

As they walked through the 1.6 million-square-foot terminal, huge windows spanned across the front and back of the expansive structure. Gold-colored panels of imperial grandeur covered the geometric folded ceilings, reminiscent of the embellished steeples found in many of the churches in St. Petersburg.

"This airport is massive. I've never seen anything like it."

"It's one of the largest. It was renovated a couple years ago. It even has a children's playground on the fourth floor." Her thoughts drifted to Jayden and how much she already missed her daughter. "Is this your first time in Russia?"

He nodded. "I heard you back there. I didn't know you speak Russian."

"It's something I picked up during my travels. It's come in handy a few times."

Hal smiled. "I'm sure it has. What time is your contact meeting us?"

Raina peered at her watch. "In about ten minutes."

She prayed Vladimir Sokolov wasn't playing games because she was running out of people she could trust. The only way this was going to work was if Vladimir was honest with her—if he knew what was good for him.

As they strolled past the numerous shops and cafes, her growling stomach reminded her how little she ate of her meal on the plane. What she needed more than anything was more sleep, not like the five hours of broken sleep she'd managed to get on the plane. She calculated she had spent thirty-four hours in the air between her flight from Bangkok and the flight to St. Petersburg.

She spotted Vladimir standing by the large glass doors at the front of the airport wearing a gray parka with a fur collar. The man didn't act or look like a typical arms dealer, at least not like the ones underground or on the black market she had dealt with in the past. He was an attractive man in his mid-fifties with dark curly hair, soft brown eyes and olive skin, who usually dressed like a Russian playboy in tailored suits and expensive silk.

Raina pointed. "That's him."

"I hope this guy is on the up and up. I don't like surprises."

She hoped so too.

Vladimir smiled as they approached.

She set her luggage down next to the man.

"I'm glad to see you are alive. I saw the reports online." He kissed both her cheeks then stood back. "You look stunning, as always. I like the new look. Very chic."

"Thank you. It's good to see you."

At least the fake reports were circulating worldwide, which made her feel a little bit better, and safer. It also made her feel better about leaving Jayden behind at the safe house.

She debated if she should use Hal's real name and decided not to. "This is my friend, Jake."

Vladimir shook Hal's hand. "Welcome to St. Petersburg, my friend." He snatched up Raina's suitcase. "Come. I have a car waiting to take you to the flat."

✳✳✳

Fifteen minutes later, the driver stopped the black Mercedes Benz Sprinter Classic in front of a four-story red-brick apartment, featuring an ornate baroque and Art Nouveau façade, located in the heart of downtown St. Petersburg on Bolshaya Morskaya Ulitsa.

Raina always loved this area. The architecture on the historic street was spectacular, filled with decades of rich history.

Vladimir sat next to her in the back seat and passed her a white card with four numbers written on it, a phone number and a key. "My flat is on the second floor. You'll need this code to enter the building. If you need anything, call that number. It's my private line." He dug into his coat pocket and pulled out a set of keys. He handed them to her. "I have a rental UAZ Patriot SUV for you, parked a few minutes from here, beside St. Isaac's Cathedral."

She took the items and looked at him. "Were you able to get everything else I asked for?"

"Of course. Everything you need is inside, as per your instructions, including food, weapons, and computer equipment. The weapons are in the spare bedroom closet. A few of my men are looking into your problem at the Agency. As soon as I learn anything, I'll contact you."

Hal glanced over his shoulder. "Do you have any idea who might be behind the kill order?"

Vladimir shook his head. "I haven't heard anything on the street or through my contacts, and in my line of business, that's quite a few in various countries."

"We believe the order is coming out of Colombia," Hal said.

"That could very well be, considering the information I read on the Internet about your American mission. I will continue to help you seek the answers you require." He touched Raina's hand. "You will be safe here."

The moment he said the words, her instincts went on alert, experience, and the past dictating her reaction even though nothing in the man's body language or the conversation had told her she should worry.

"Thank you." She opened the door and looked him square in the eyes. "Remember, as far as anyone is concerned, I am dead. That includes your men. We don't need anyone going rogue. Let me know if you hear anything."

Vladimir nodded and watched her, and Hal exit the car.

The driver removed their luggage from the trunk and handed the bags to them.

As they walked to the front door, Raina peered over her shoulder and watched the Mercedes drive away. The icy mid-afternoon air made her eyes water and sent a chill through her.

Hal pulled his winter coat closed. "The guy certainly wasn't what I was expecting for an arms dealer. Not even close. We had better not be walking into a trap."

She looked up at the building and drew a deep breath. "I hope not."

CHAPTER EIGHT

The sun lowered, spreading an array of fiery shades of pink and orange across the horizon. Hal put the key in the lock and turned. He glanced behind him. "Ready?"

Raina nodded.

He opened the door then went in and checked all the rooms. "It's clear."

He saw the relief in her eyes when she realized Vladimir hadn't double-crossed them.

Inside, the space was large, open and airy, with beige walls and shiny light-colored wooden floors. The decor was elegant, simple and uncluttered.

Again, not what Hal had expected because Vladimir seemed more like a luxury kind of guy. "This is his spare apartment?"

She put her shoulder bag and luggage down then took off her boots. "He has a house just outside of St. Petersburg. Actually, a mansion that looks like a castle and a few other properties." She walked around the living room. "I think he uses this apartment for some of his business transactions."

He took off his coat and tossed it on the back of

the couch. "At least there weren't a bunch of Russians waiting to kill us. So far, your friend has been true to his word."

"As much as I don't want to believe he would cross us, I'm not taking any chances. If it's one thing I've learned, things can change in an instant, especially if you let your guard down."

She was right. He'd seen it happen dozens of times. Hal sat on the couch and pulled off his boots, his body weary from the long flight. "Did you want to sleep for a while? You must be exhausted."

"I'm okay, but I think I'll take a shower, then we should get to work. I want this problem fixed so I can go back to my daughter."

He could only imagine how much she missed Jayden. "Sounds good."

While Raina took a shower, Hal sat and turned on one of the two laptops sitting on a long desk by the living room window. He pulled his cell phone from his shirt pocket and made a quick call to Angela.

"Hello."

It was good to hear her voice. "How you doing, Donahue?"

"Better. I want to go home."

"Not for a few days yet. Not until we're certain the latest threat is looked after. For now, you're staying put. You're safe. The US Marshal Service has your back."

"I love the way you're always looking out for me. I just wish you could come to visit and bring me a smoke."

Hal laughed. "Not going to happen for a couple days. By that time, you won't want a cigarette."

"Yeah, you're probably right."

There was a long pause on the other end before she spoke again.

"Are you any closer to finding out who wants us dead?"

He glanced around the apartment and frowned. He felt bad he was lying to her, not keeping her in the loop. He'd never done that before, and he didn't like it. It was for her own good, he kept telling himself.

"No, but Raina and I are following up on a lead. Hopefully soon." He heard muffled voices in the background.

"I have to go. The bloody vampires want to take more blood to make sure my leg isn't infected. Like they haven't taken enough. I've been running a fever the last few hours."

"Better to have it checked. I'll give you a call tomorrow. Check up on you."

"Thanks. Stay safe and watch your back."

After he ended the call, Hal looked at the laptop screen. That didn't sound good. He hoped there wasn't any infection. That was the last thing she needed. Being shot was more than enough to deal with.

He rubbed the back of his neck and searched online for his and Raina's names. A morbid image of a mangled car wrapped around a tree popped up. A chill spiked down his spine. He read the headline:

Ex-FBI Agent and Former CIA Agent Killed in Grisly Car Wreck Months After Secret US Mission to Colombia

Hal didn't need to read any further, didn't want to know all the details of his fabricated death but he did notice the words 'fire and decapitation'. Chambers had done a good job faking their deaths. He just hoped their demise would be believed. He let out a deep breath. He didn't know where to start. They didn't know who the task force leak was, no idea who had put out the kill order, and no clue how they were going to deal with it. The only thing Hal did know—the threat was going to end.

He heard the shower shut off. Minutes later, Raina appeared, looking refreshed, wearing black yoga pants and a black tank top and carrying a gun in each hand.

"I checked out the weapons stash." She handed Hal one of the guns. "That's a PL-14 pistol. You'll like it. Short recoil and trigger pull. Used by the Russian army. Vladimir must have had a special on them."

He held the pistol and smiled, amazed by how much she knew about weapons. "What's that one?"

"GSh-18. It's light. Recoil-operated with a double-feed system. The trigger is like a Glock, and the sights have a white-dot for faster aiming."

He'd seen the woman in action. He knew what she could do. "Not that you'd need it." Glocks, Berettas and sniper rifles were his thing. "What other Russian goodies did your friend bring?"

"AK-9 assault rifles, HK MP7 machine guns, grenades, C4, binoculars, headsets, vests, and extra outwear, coats and hats."

Vladimir had thought of everything, including outerwear for the huge difference in temperature compared to Las Vegas. Hal never liked the cold and he was grateful for the additional warm clothing. But with an inventory like that, he wasn't sure what the guy thought they were going to do. Storm the Agency?

While Raina was busy in the kitchen, making them toasted bacon, tomato, and cheese sandwiches, Hal searched online for information about the Agency and found a recent article by a popular and trusted US magazine.

"It says here the estimated number of employees is about four hundred, working in various departments on twelve hours shifts from nine to nine." He kept reading. "And the Agency has a budget of at least four hundred thousand dollars US per month. That's one hell of a budget to spread propaganda."

"It's big business, circulating rumors. It has been for decades. Feeding on hate pays." Raina set one of two plates with sandwiches and freshly cut fruit next to him and a bottle of beer. She took a seat beside him at the desk and popped a piece of pineapple in her mouth.

"The unidentified person in the article said she worked in something called the Elite Special Projects department while other workers spent their day pumping out anti-western and pro-Kremlin comments on the most popular social media sites." Hal took a big bite of his sandwich and washed it down with a gulp of beer.

Raina's cell phone went off. She hopped out of the chair and grabbed her shoulder bag. She pulled out her phone and paused for a moment. "It's a text message from Vladimir—and a picture of a twenty-something-year-old Russian named Demayan Chuchnova. According to Vladimir, the man works at the Agency and might have some information for us."

She glanced up at Hal. "If he is persuaded."

He could play the persuasion game. Hal took another bite of his sandwich and checked his watch. "I guess we know what we're doing tonight."

CHAPTER NINE

At eight-thirty, Hal and Raina picked up the black rental SUV parked west of the cathedral. Even at night, the outside of the Russian Orthodox basilica was stunning with its magnificent colorful mosaic panels depicting scenes from the New Testament.

She glanced at Hal then back to the road. "You really need to see inside. It has a gold-plated dome that rises three hundred feet, and underneath the peak are sculpted white doves representing the Holy Spirit. It's as if you're looking straight up into heaven. It's breathtakingly beautiful."

"Sounds like it, but I don't think we're going to have any time for sightseeing. We have to be on the return flight in less than six hours. That doesn't give us much time to do what we need to do as it is. Kind of wish we did have time, though. The outside of the cathedral is spectacular."

Raina steered the SUV right and drove east toward Savushkina Street.

The streets were surprisingly quiet. Light snow fell and disintegrated the moment the small flakes touched the windshield. The SUV's headlights bounced back and forth across the road and laminated the barren sidewalks.

She gripped the steering wheel with both hands and leaned forward, trying to read the numbers on the outside of the buildings. "There it is." She pointed. "Number fifteen." She drove past the structure and turned around farther down the street, wanting to park across from the Agency so they could watch for the man they sought.

"Doesn't look like much, considering their huge operating budget." Hal laughed. "Got to love the sign out front. Business Centre."

"Slightly deceiving, considering the lies they're spreading across the world from inside." She parked under a streetlight and shut off the headlights then looked across the street.

The four-story modern building was nothing special, built with bland-looking beige-colored granite and large brown-trimmed windows. To anyone who didn't know what the building was, it just looked like an office complex.

"What do you want to do? Grab him and see what info we can get out of him?" Raina asked/

"Yeah. We're going to have to. We'll take him for a drive. See what we can learn." Hal reached into his backpack, pulled out two black balaclavas, and passed one to her.

She glanced at the digital clock on the dash and shut off the engine not wanting to look suspicious. "They should start coming out in about five minutes. It's going to be hard to figure out which parking lot he's going to go to with one on both sides of the building."

"That's okay. We'll run him off the road if we have to. I don't really want to grab him in front of a bunch of witnesses."

Raina agreed. It would be too risky with others around.

While they waited, she had a hard time fighting off the overwhelming exhaustion creeping to take over. She unrolled the window part-way down, trusting that the frosty night air would keep her wide awake and focused. Cold air seeped throughout the car and chilled her skin. "There he is. In the brown leather bomber jacket."

"Let's see where he goes."

Raina watched through the tinted glass and observed the man wave to another employee then turned and headed down the sidewalk. He pulled out a black wool hat from his coat pocket and put it on.

"He didn't drive to work. Looks like we just got lucky."

"It will be much easier this way." She started the engine and waited for the long stream of vehicles to leave the parking lot. "Can you still see him?"

"Yeah. He's about three-quarters of the way up the block." Hal pulled the balaclava over his head and adjusted it.

Raina did the same, then put the SUV in drive and turned on the headlights. She pulled out slowly.

"Stay back until the traffic in the other direction is clear." Hal grabbed the PL-14 pistol from his coat pocket.

She glanced in the rear-view mirror and then to the bright headlights coming at them in the opposite direction.

Hal turned in the seat and watched the taillights

disappear. "We're good."

She pressed down the accelerator and came to a screeching stop a few yards ahead of the man.

Hal threw open the door and jumped out.

Raina smiled to herself. Hal's size alone would scare anyone.

The man froze, clearly not sure what was going on until he saw Hal's gun. His jaw dropped open.

Hal opened the back door and gave the man a shove. "Get in."

Her eyes traveled to the rear-view mirror, and she spotted headlights.

Hal pushed the man, and he tumbled head-first into the back seat. Hal hopped in and slammed the door shut.

She stomped the gas pedal and turned right at the next street.

"Who are you?" the man asked.

"You speak English. Great. We just got lucky twice in one night, Demayan Chuchnova."

"How do you know my name?"

Hal kept the gun aimed at the man's chest and heard the fear in the man's voice.

Raina passed her cell phone over the seat to Hal with the details from Vladimir's text message.

"We know quite a bit about you. You're the head of the Special Projects department, who posts specific fake articles on dozens of social media sites. Remember this one?" He shoved the phone in the man's face.

"Yes, why?"

"Who told you to post it? I want a name. Otherwise, my friend here is going to take you to an old warehouse and get the information we want the hard way if you know what I mean."

The man didn't answer.

Hal waited a few minutes then said, "Driver. Head south to the warehouse. We're going to do this the hard way."

Raina nodded.

"Wait!" Demayan hesitated for a second and twisted his hands in his lap. "My boss told me to go meet with a man about a special project involving Americans. He said we would split a large bonus if I helped him and didn't tell any of the other employees about it."

"Who's the man you met?"

"He said his name was Alejandro—something. I can't remember."

Her heart skipped a beat. Alejandro Quintero was alive? He never died in the explosion at Pablo Sanchez's compound in Bogotá? She glanced in the rear-view mirror then back to the road. But what was the Colombian doing in Russia?

"Where did you meet him?"

"At a house in St. Petersburg."

"What's the address?"

"I—can't remember."

"Think," Hal growled.

"It's the sixth house east of the Belizia Kafe on Starodervenskaya."

"Give me your wallet and cell phone."

Demanyan plunged his hands in his pockets and shakily handed over the items.

Hal rifled through the wallet and took a picture of the man's ID with his phone. "I have your address and phone number. As of now, we're going to be working on a secret project together." He handed the phone and wallet back to Demanyan. "I'll be in contact in a few hours. And Demanyan—if you don't do exactly as you're told, we will make sure that you take that trip to the warehouse. You'd be amazed at what my friend here can do to a human body. Pretty sickening. Driver. We're done here.

Raina slowed the SUV and steered to the side of the road and stopped.

Hal stuck the gun in the man's face. "Now get out. If you tell anyone about anything that happened here tonight—you're dead. Got it?"

The man shook his head rapidly then scrambled out of the vehicle, half-tripping, trying to keep his balance.

She watched him run down the sidewalk and disappear around the corner. She yanked off the balaclava and tossed it on the passenger seat, her face moist with perspiration. "Alejandro Quintero is here in St. Petersburg. That's a hard one to swallow, considering we all thought he was killed in the blast."

Hal shook his head. "He's must have been offsite."

Now with one of the cartel's higher-ups apparently alive, Raina couldn't help but wonder if Abdul Shakra, the terrorist who'd orchestrated the attack at Diablo Canyon was alive, as well. The thought drove a shiver down her spine. She prayed Jayden was safe. She had to believe she was.

"Any idea how far the Belizia Kafe is from here?" Hal asked.

Raina had never heard of the place. She punched the name into the onboard GPS. "It's about fifteen minutes away."

"Good. Time to do a little reconnaissance."

CHAPTER TEN

As they drove past the Belizia Kafe, Hal grabbed the night vision binoculars from the backpack on the back seat and counted the houses as they passed. He pointed. "That must be it."

Raina parked the SUV two houses down from the modern two-story house with a roof like a church steeple. She shut off the engine.

He hoped for Demayan Chuchnova's sake, the man wasn't leading them on a wild goose chase or into a trap. Hal had already called Chambers to see if he could find out who owned the house. He needed as much information as possible before he put his and Raina's life on the line, especially if they decided they were going to storm the place. Just because Alejandro Quintero had survived the bomb blast in Colombia didn't mean the bastard would survive the night. Stopping him would put a halt to the propaganda he'd been paying to have fed through the Agency.

Raina unzipped her coat part-way. "It looks like the place was built recently compared to the other houses on the street."

"You're right. It doesn't look very old."

An upstairs light turned on.

Hal peered through the binoculars and watched a man walk in front of the window and close the curtains. "Someone's home." He passed the binoculars to her.

"There are probably others. I can't imagine Quintero not having a few men with him. For all we know, there could be a dozen. I still don't understand why he's in Russia."

"Me neither but we're going to find out. How do you want to play this, since we haven't heard back from Chambers yet?"

She lowered the binoculars and looked at him. "Quick and dirty. We don't even know if there's a security system."

"Guns blazing?"

"I don't think we have a choice. We'll have to take our chances."

It was risky with the houses so close together. All it would take was one nosy neighbor, and they'd be spending their time inside a Russian jail, probably somewhere in Siberia.

She reached behind her and seized the backpack from the back seat. She passed him a headset and put hers on. After a quick test to ensure the older Russian equipment worked, Hal double-checked his weapon.

"Wait. Someone just came out the front door." Raina picked up the binoculars. "A man. He's having a cigarette. He just walked around to the side of the house."

"This is our chance." Hal opened the door and hopped out. The cold air bit his face and reminded him how he wished he was back in the warmth of Las

Vegas.

He looked up and down the street. All was quiet, and he prayed it would stay that way. He ran across the street. Raina followed hum.

"Do you see anyone else around?' Hal's earpiece crackled, and he adjusted it.

She looped the straps of the backpack over her shoulders. "No. Just him."

"We have to do this as quietly as possible."

Hal ran to the corner of the house and stopped. He peeked around the corner.

The man was leaning against the house. Smoke curled up around his head and drifted in the night air.

Hal raised the PL-14 and pussyfooted along the wall. When he reached the man, he seized him by the back of the neck and jabbed the barrel of the gun into his back.

Raina stood in front of the man and pointed her gun in his face.

The man flinched and started speaking in Russian.

"What's he saying?" Hal looked at Raina.

"He's a doctor. He claims he is here to visit a friend."

She continued to talk to the man in Russian.

The man tossed his cigarette at his feet and squashed it with the heel of his boot.

Raina glanced at Hal. "There are two men in the living room and a sick man upstairs."

Hal figured it might be Alejandro Quintero who was upstairs. "Ask him if the living room is at the front of the house or the back."

She stared at the man and asked him. "He says it's in the back."

Hal let go of the man's neck and glanced up at the

house next door to make sure no one was watching through the windows. "Tell him to start walking to the front door. He's getting us inside."

As the man slowly walked ahead of him, Hal observed that he walked with a slight limp. He kept his gun pointed at the doctor's back, in spite of the fact he was sure the man wasn't going to do anything stupid that would get him killed.

A gray cat scurried past them and ran under the car parked in the driveway. The animal poked his head out then disappeared.

"Tell him if he says a word, or alerts anyone inside, a bullet is going to shatter his spine. Make sure he understands."

Raina translated what Hal said.

The man nodded, his eyes wide and alert with fear.

Apparently, the guy had gotten the message loud and clear. Hal didn't want to shoot the man, but he would, if necessary. He snatched the doctor by the neck again and glanced at Raina. "Ready?"

She nodded and opened the door.

The doctor stepped inside and stopped.

Hal flicked on the foyer light as Raina two-handed the GSh-18 and walked ahead of them a few feet. He heard muffled voices and what sounded like a Russian TV show blaring from the back of the house. His eyes snapped to the dark room to his right. He whispered into the mic. "Check the kitchen."

Raina crouched and disappeared around the corner.

Seconds later, he heard her in his earpiece. "It's clear. I'm going to go and take care of the problem in the back."

Hal knew she was more than capable and could take out the men with speed and accuracy before they knew what hit them. "Be careful." He licked his lips, and his eyes shifted to the dining room that appeared empty and then at the stairs. "I'll head up with the doctor."

With each step, the wooden stairs creaked.

At the top, Hal stopped and heard two loud pops.

Raina's voice filled his ear. "It's taken care of."

He gave the doctor a shove in the direction of the master bedroom at the end of the hall. They probably didn't have a lot of time.

Raina came up behind them. "I checked the rest of the house. There are no other issues. We need to hurry."

Hal nodded then followed the doctor into the master bedroom.

The large room was set up like a hospital suite, complete with a half-dozen pieces of medical equipment. Medication was spread out on a small table in the corner.

Alejandro Quintero lay, propped up on a king-size bed with an IV in his arm. His head was bald, and the right side of his face was covered with red blisters and black lacerations, his face almost unrecognizable from the photographs Hal had seen of the man.

"He *was* at the blast site. They look like radiation burns." Hal lowered his gun.

The man was far from a threat. He was frail and looked as if he were dying. If anything, Hal would be doing the bastard a favor, putting him out of his misery by killing him.

She kept her gun aimed at Quintero's head. "The doctor said he has treated many patients during and after Chernobyl. Quintero was brought to Russia to be treated. He has third and fourth beta radiation burns and chronic radiation keratosis. Cancer."

"Ask him if he knows who brought him here."

She turned to the doctor again and asked him.

"He said he was brought by the man who owns the house, but he doesn't know his name."

Recognition flickered in the back of Quintero's brown eyes, and he stared hard at Hal. He spoke through blistered, swollen lips. "I know who you both are. You can change your looks, but that won't save either of you. Many in the cartel will come for you, and they will kill you."

"Well, I don't think we have to worry about that anymore. I guess you didn't see the news online. We're already dead. We died in a horrible car accident. The game is over." He shoved his gun into his coat pocket. "Take the doc to the hallway. I'll look after Quintero."

She nodded and gave the doctor a helpful nudge with her gun. "He's all yours."

After Raina left, Hal yanked one of the pillows out from under Quintero's head. "You killed a lot of people—a lot of innocent people. Many are still suffering and will be for a long time." His thoughts turned to his friend, Oscar, who had helped stop the second attack. He'd still be alive if it wasn't for Quintero and Abdul Shakra. He held the pillow above the man's head.

Spit dribbled from the corner of the man's mouth. "I'm glad many died. That was the purpose of the attack at the nuclear facility. It will happen again, and next time, tens of thousands will perish." Quintero smirked and shook his head. "Killing me won't stop anything. The wheels are already in motion, as you Americans say. They have been—for months."

Another attack had already been planned? Worry worked through him and his stomach tightened into a tight ball. Hal clenched his jaw, and the muscles in his arms flinched. He lowered the pillow over the man's face and pressed. He held the pillow down with all his strength.

Quintero kicked and thrashed and tried to scratch Hal's arms, but he was too weak. Finally, after a few minutes, the man's limbs went limp, and the heart monitor's alarm went off.

He removed the pillow, grabbed his cell phone from his back pocket, and snapped a picture of the dead man's face. Then he heard a car door slam shut.

Hal hurried to the window and peered outside.

Four men climbed out of a van parked across the street and walked toward the front of the house.

He rushed out of the room and met Raina in the hallway. "We've got company."

She pulled a grenade out of the backpack and hooked the strap of the pack over her shoulder. Her gaze shifted to the doctor then back to Hal. "What about him?"

If he left the doctor here, he would be killed. Hal didn't want the man's death on his conscience. He did nothing wrong except for look after a man who was responsible for the deaths of thousands and probably knew nothing, other than what he had been ordered to do. "Take him with us. We'll dump him along the way. Go out the back."

Their heavy footsteps hammered down the stairs and they ran through the house. Hal threw open the back door. Frigid cold air greeted them. He looked over his shoulder and saw the men: four hefty Russians, carrying machine guns with determined looks on their faces.

Raina removed the safety ring on the grenade and pulled the pin. She bent and tossed it inside the door.

The grenade bounced and rolled toward the men.

She snagged the doctor's arm and tugged. "Move!"

They barely had enough time to make it into the neighbor's yard when the back door blew off the house with a thunderous bang. Glass shattered. Lights flicked on in the adjacent houses.

"We have to get out of here before the authorities show up." Hal snatched the doctor's other arm and they raced to the SUV.

Once they were inside the vehicle, Raina rammed the keys in the ignition and stomped the accelerator.

CHAPTER ELEVEN

Back at Vladimir's apartment, Raina threw her things into her suitcase and zipped it up. "The doctor didn't look happy about being dumped in the middle of nowhere."

"I know. I didn't want him to know where we were going. He'd already witnessed enough to get us arrested," Hal said.

She felt relieved, knowing that Alejandro Quintero was finally dead, but she was worried. "Do you think he was telling the truth, that another attack is already in motion?"

He scratched his head. "I don't know what to think. Could be just words from a man who knew he was about to die. On the other hand, after what happened at Diablo Canyon, we have to take it seriously regardless if it's true or not."

"Check this out." He handed her his cell phone.

She read the headline on the screen:

Colombia's Sur del Calle Cartel Leader Alejandro Quintero Dead After Being Treated for Radiation Burns in St. Petersburg, Russia

Raina stared at the photograph of the man's disfigured face for a long moment. She was grateful Hal had killed him. If he hadn't, she certainly would have. "Our Agency friend, Demayan Chuchnova posted this?" She passed him back his phone.

"I emailed him the picture. He really didn't have a choice, though. I told him if he didn't post the article immediately, you and I were going to pay him a visit at his home. Amazing what a little power of persuasion can do."

She smiled. With Alejandro out of the picture and their fake deaths trending on the Internet, Raina could relax, knowing she and Jayden were safe. Another threat eliminated. The second her body began to relax, she realized how exhausted she was and how much she needed to sleep. They still had a few hours before their flight back to Las Vegas, and she couldn't wait to be back in the US with her daughter.

Hal's phone went off. "Yeah?" He listened intently for a moment. "Really?" He glanced at Raina and frowned. "Are you sure? Okay. We'll leave now." He shoved the phone into the back pocket of his pants.

"What's wrong? Is Jayden okay? Angela?"

"They're both fine." He shook his head and started gathering his personal items and throwing them in his suitcase. "We need to leave. That was Chambers." He grabbed his weapon and the backpack. "That house where Alejandro Quintero was staying belongs to your friend, Vladimir. I'm guessing he and his men are probably on the way here now that he knows Quintero is dead."

Anger bubbled inside her. She snatched the handle

of her suitcase and dropped it on the floor by her feet. The man had lied to her, just like Chakan Aawut had done. "Why did he help us by giving us Demayan Chuchnova's name at the Agency? It doesn't make sense if he had planned on killing us anyway."

"Maybe Quintero offered him something on his deathbed that Vladimir couldn't refuse. Perhaps a lot more than the thirty-million-dollar bounty on our heads, maybe an arms deal with the Colombian cartel that he couldn't turn down. All I know is, we're still in danger."

While Hal threw on his coat, Raina tossed on her jacket and slipped her gun in the pocket. If Hal was right, she'd have to kill Vladimir. She had no choice. She couldn't let him live and continue to be a threat to her and Jayden. She rushed to the window and pushed back the corner of the blinds. Vladimir's black Mercedes Benz pulled up and parked a couple of car lengths in front of the SUV.

"He's here. So far, it looks like it's him and three of his men."

They grabbed their belongings and hustled down the apartment stairs.

After finding the back exit, Hal and Raina sprinted around the building and to the SUV. She hid behind the vehicle and dropped the backpack. After digging through the bag, she pulled out two rectangles of C4. She didn't have a detonator and would have to make do with what she had available.

While Vladimir and his man walked through the double front doors of the apartment building, she ran and smacked the sticky side of the putty-like explosives directly on the back bumper of the Mercedes. She high-tailed it back to the SUV and threw her things inside then jumped into the driver seat. Hal was sitting in the passenger seat with a confused expression on his face.

He raised an eyebrow. "We're going to hit it?"

She jammed the keys into the ignition, ready the moment her adversaries were in the vehicle. "Without a detonator, we'll have to use the impact of the SUV smashing into the bumper. It's going to have to be a hard hit. Hopefully, it will create enough friction to produce some heat and enough of a shockwave to set off the explosives." She slung the seatbelt over her shoulder and locked it in place. "Buckle up."

Her heart thumped, and adrenaline raced through her veins. This had better work. The timing would have to be perfect. She glanced up at the apartment window and saw Vladimir looking outside. Thanks to the darkly tinted windows in the SUV, he couldn't see them.

Hal threw on his seatbelt and placed his gun on his lap. "Let's hope it works."

Minutes later, she spotted Vladimir hurrying out the front door. He stopped and glanced up and down the street before he and his men headed to the Mercedes.

Raina inhaled a long breath and exhaled, her fingers on the keys, ready to start the SUV.

Once Vladimir and his men were inside the car, she started the engine, threw the SUV into drive and floored the accelerator.

Tires squealed.

The force of the crash shoved the Mercedes into the car parked in front of it with a loud bang.

Raina's body jerked forward, the seatbelt taut against her chest and neck. The front airbags deployed. The thin, nylon fabric belted her in the face. Her head flopped back and smacked the headrest. She shoved the airbag down toward her legs out of the way and drove the vehicle into reverse and then floored the gas pedal. The tires spun and kicked up a trail of smoke and exhaust. When she was at a safe distance, she stopped the SUV and waited.

Hal looked at her. "Do you think it—"

An ear-piecing explosion rocked the SUV.

The back of the Mercedes lifted twenty feet off the ground and smashed down on the road. The trunk blew off, rocketed into the air, and took out one of the streetlights before landing on the sidewalk. Yellowy-orange-blue flames fanned out beneath the car and spread up the side of the vehicle. Within seconds, the car was engulfed with Vladimir and his men trapped inside.

"I guess it worked." Hal checked the side-view mirror. "Let's get the hell out of here."

Raina smiled to herself, satisfied Vladimir was no longer a threat. She drew a long deep breath then cranked the wheel and steered the SUV toward the airport.

CHAPTER TWELVE

Las Vegas, Nevada

"Momma! Momma!" Jayden raced down the safe house hallway in bare feet dressed in her favorite pink dress covered with multi-colored butterflies.

Raina bent and held out her arms. Her daughter ran and leapt into her arms. Raina hugged her for a long moment then kissed her forehead. "Oh, baby. I have missed you *so* much." She looked at Robson. "No other problems since we've been gone?"

"None at all after the compromise. Jayden and Russler and I had a great time. Bet you didn't know your daughter is one heck of a Fish player. She's a pro."

Raina laughed and put Jayden down. She was relieved to hear there were no further threats. The knot in her stomach vanished.

"Come on, Jayden. Let's get a sandwich for lunch and then go watch a movie," Robson said.

Her daughter followed the man to the kitchen, skipping all the way.

Hal brought in their luggage and set it on the floor. He swiped his hand across his forehead. Dark circles shadowed his eyes.

She stood and stretched. They were both worn out and exhausted. Too many flights in such a short amount of time. Jet-setting certainly wasn't as much fun as it sounded.

"Hey, good to see you're back." Mike smiled at her. "I heard you guys had quite the adventure."

"Not an adventure I want to do again. I think it's safe to say Hal and I are both happy to be back in the US."

"Hell, yes. At least it's warm here. Bloody freezing in Russia. Where's Russler?"

"Chambers sent him back to the office. Angela and Rambo Robot are in the kitchen. Angela wanted to be here. Be warned. She's not happy you lied to her about going to Russia."

Hal waved his hand. "Donahue will get over it—in time." He turned to Raina and whispered in her ear, "You're not going to like Chambers. Just a heads-up. He's an arrogant asshole."

She'd dealt with many men in the past like that, and she had a cure for arrogance. "That's okay. I could kill him."

Hal burst out laughing, and so did Mike. "Not a bad idea."

"I like the way she thinks," Mike said.

In the kitchen, Angela was sitting in a wheelchair at the table. A white cast covered her leg.

Her eyes lit up when she saw Hal. "Nice hair, Decker."

Hal grinned and ran his hand through his hair. "Now, don't you start." He bent and kissed her cheek.

Raina felt the chemistry going on between the two, even though Hal had said they were only friends. A near-death experience could do that to people. She wouldn't be surprised if they were a couple in the near future. "It's good to see you, Angela."

"You too, Raina. I'm glad you guys are back safe and sound."

Mike sat beside Angela and took a sip of his beer.

Raina stared at the gray-haired man dressed in a black suit and red tie, leaning against the kitchen counter with his ankles crossed and a beer in his hand. He had FBI written all over him.

"Raina, this is Trent Chambers," Hal said.

Chambers held out his hand. "It's good to finally meet you. Hal and Angela have a lot of good things to say about you—considering."

Hal was right. The guy was arrogant. Raina forced herself to shake the man's hand.

Hal rolled his eyes and went to the fridge. He grabbed two cans of beers and opened them. He passed one to Raina then pulled out a chair for her.

She sat down and heard Jayden's bubbly laughter echoing from the living room. She smiled to herself, and her heart squeezed. It was the best sound in the world to hear her child happy.

Chambers uncrossed his legs. "We were finally able to confirm who our task force leak is. Nicolas Artur."

Hal's eyes widened. "Christ, he's the last person I would have thought would be involved." He shook his head. "I can't believe it. What's the connection between him, Vladimir and Quintero?"

"Artur and Vladimir were childhood friends. He'd spent his early years in Russia before his family moved to the US when he was sixteen. When Artur got himself into a mob-related gambling debt, over three million dollars to be exact, and couldn't dig his way out, he reached out to his old friend who'd been working with Quintero and the cartel for decades dealing arms. I would have never thought he was the leak, either. He's been with the Bureau for close to fourteen years. One of our best agents."

Raina didn't regret for one second killing Vladimir. He'd gotten what he deserved, along with Quintero. Raina glanced up at Chambers. "Quintero wanted revenge against us for stopping the dirty bomb in Colombia, and Vladimir probably fell into a windfall for his involvement, either by cash or an extra-special weapons deal. Then he got greedier, decided why not kill us and collect the thirty-million-dollar bounty since Quintero's health was rapidly going downhill."

Chambers nodded. "Sounds about right."

"And it was Artur who gave the entry codes for the safe house to Quintero, and he passed them to his local cartel contacts. Artur hit the jackpot and got his debt to the mob paid in full," Mike added.

"It's always about money. Anyway, I have to get back to the Bureau." Chambers set his empty can on the counter. "Homeland Security and our offices are on high alert in case what Quintero had said is true and another attack is imminent."

"Let's hope to hell the bastard was lying, for all our sakes," Hal said.

Raina couldn't agree more. The last attack was devastating enough.

After Chambers left, she looked up and saw Robson standing in the doorway with Jayden standing beside him.

He shoved his hands into his pants pockets. "My twins' birthday party is tomorrow. My wife and I would like you and Jayden to come if you can. I know my girls would love it."

"Can we go?" Jayden asked. "Please, Momma."

How could she say no? "Of course. We would love to come to the party."

"Oh, before I forget, a friend of mine has a nice house for rent here in Las Vegas. It's yours if you're interested in staying," Mike said.

She would like nothing more than to have some normalcy in her life and Jayden's life. She could get her daughter back into school, where the child could socialize with other children, instead of always being on the run and living a lonely existence. But there was something Raina needed to do first.

She glanced at Robson. "Would you and your wife mind watching Jayden after the birthday party for about forty-eight hours? I have something I have to do."

There was no way Chakan Aawut was going to get away with what he had done. Jayden could have been killed. His betrayal would cost him everything. She would make sure the man suffered in more ways than he could imagine before she put a bullet in his head.

"We'd love to. Take whatever time you need," Robson said.

While Raina thought about Mike's house offer for a few more minutes, she glanced at him, and then to Hal, Angela, and Robson. She was grateful for their friendship. It felt good to be finally home. "When can I see the house?"

Author's Note

I hope you enjoyed reading *Dawn of the Enemy*.

To my fans, readers, and reviewers—thank you!
You rock!

The story was originally published in 2015 featuring
JET from Russell Blake's *New York Times* and *USA
Today* bestselling action thriller series.
The story recently reworked with a new kick-ass
character, Raina Storm, who will also be appearing in
the fourth Whitney Steel novel: *Redemption*.

Can't wait for more Raina Storm?

Enjoy an excerpt from Deadly Shadow
(The Assassin Chronicles – Book One)

DEADLY SHADOW

The Assassin Chronicles – Book One

Kim Cresswell

KC Publishing
Ontario, Canada

KC Publishing
London, Ontario Canada

Publisher's Note: This is a work of fiction. Names, characters, places, and incidents are a product of the author's imagination. Locales and public names are sometimes used for atmospheric purposes. Any resemblance to actual people, living or dead, or to businesses, companies, events, institutions, or locales is completely coincidental.

Cover Art © 2018

Ordering Information:
Quantity sales. Special discounts are available on quantity purchases by corporations, associations, and others. For details, contact the publisher at the address above.

Deadly Shadow/Kim Cresswell. – 1st edition.
ISBN 978-0-9950578-5-2

CHAPTER ONE

Within the hour, Derrick Lynn would kill his next target, a popular radio host known as 'Big Mouth' Bullington. He didn't want or need any specifics about the target, only who and when. He'd learned a long time ago to keep that distance to make his job a lot easier to deal with. Never women or children. Never a non-target—which at times took an incredible amount of self-control. More than anyone could imagine.

Like his grandfather and father, he could move about in real-time, watching people and events while his physical body remained asleep. The paranormal freaks called it etheric travel. But his real gift was psychokinesis, a gift very few in the world had. He used his mind to move objects. It came in damn handy, turning anything and everything into a deadly weapon.

For over twenty years he'd evaded the authorities—in particular, FBI Agent Victory McClane. And he was hell-bent on keeping it that way, no matter the cost.

In the large soundproof bedroom, Derrick laid on his back in his king-size bed, looking up at the ceiling with his hands clasped behind his head. Silk sheets covered his legs and, barely, his groin. The only light in the room came from the eerie glow radiating from the cell phone cradled in its charger on the nightstand next to his laptop. He glanced at the studio headshot of Eddie Bullington filling the phone's screen as the podcast of the man's radio show played at mid-volume.

"... and while it's a bunch of bull that Republicans work to keep the Black man down..."

His eyes shifted to the bathroom doorway to his dinner companion, Alessandra, a thirty-something runway model with long blonde hair and voguish features. She straightened her white blouse over her black skirt then put her hoop earrings back on. Alessandra shot him a soft smile and grabbed the silver faux-fur coat laying on the end of the bed. Before leaving she bent and kissed him, her lips warm against his. Derrick closed his eyes as Bullington's podcast droned on.

"... if you think the Dems are squeaky clean then I've got some prime Louisiana property for you. Those Limousine Liberals keep their boots pressed against the back of our necks, pretending to be on the side of equality and justice..."

He inhaled and exhaled slowly a dozen times and visualized his target's bedroom. His body felt light, floating. Before losing consciousness, he jerked himself awake, then let himself go under again. Deeper into a half-sleep state, he felt as if he were bobbing in a boat. As the rocking intensified, high-pitched ringing sounded in his ears and his limbs vibrated and buzzed like a bee's nest. He left the physical plane, his astral body flying.

✳ ✳ ✳

Eddie Bullington stood in the shower. Steaming hot water pulsated hard against the back of his shoulder blades. The "*God Bless America*" Muzak-like ringtone blasted from the phone sitting on the counter next to the double sink. He shut the water off, stepped out of the shower stall, and grabbed his regal-looking red and gold bathrobe from the back of the door. He quickly slipped it on and answered the call.

"Let me guess, Sid. You want to talk about last week's show."

"Sure do. Ratings are down five-percent from last quarter. That's a cause for concern."

"Just relax, okay? Anything else or are you going to keep on complaining about the same old thing?"

"Five-percent is a big deal, Eddie."

"Go to bed, Sid. I got this. I'll be in a little earlier than usual for the show." Eddie disconnected and shook his head.

His producer, Sid Moller, was a pain on a good day. Eddie didn't feel like dealing with the man's silliness. His ratings were fine. He was still the top radio host in the United States, his shows syndicated on four continents.

With the phone clutched in his hand, he strolled

barefoot into the spacious antechamber located next to his bedroom and flopped down into the extra-wide recliner. After setting the phone on the end table he picked up the TV remote, along with a half bag of Cheetos. Eddie flicked on the TV to watch the latest episode of *"Tucker Carlson Tonight"* and dug into the snack bag.

* * *

Derrick's eyelids fluttered. Blackness. Then a long, dark tunnel emerged and grew wider. Sounds, natural and alien, came and went as a frantic rush of lights, faces, and places blazed toward him. He bobbed and weaved. Images, some distinct, others not, warped and flew toward him, through him, past him. The sounds and images intensified. Then they stopped. He was in Bullington's bedroom.

* * *

Derrick stood behind Eddie, his naked body blurry and silhouetted in shadow. The room was filled with over-stuffed antique furniture, gaudy gold and green patterned drapes, and a Victorian rug in various hideous shades of red and pink. A mounted rhinoceros head glared down at it all.

His eyes shifted to the end table, then to Eddie's phone. He trembled. Sweat dripped from his forehead and ran down the sides of his face. His gaze moved to the colorful ad for gold on the TV screen while the male announcer excitedly implored viewers to act now because there has never been a better time to buy. Derrick directed his energy at the end table drawer. It quietly eased open. Inside was a Baby Glock. He concentrated harder, staring, focusing as much energy as he could at the weapon.

The gun twitched. And turned. And rose from the drawer. The barrel moved within an inch from Bullington's right temple.

Eddie twisted his head as if sensing something was about to happen. "What the—"

An angry gunshot cracked.

Blood, bone, and brain matter splattered and sprayed across the room. Various colored fluids and small lumps ran down the TV from a splotch at the top of the screen.

Derrick grunted. The gun traveled back to the end table and the drawer slammed shut.

* * *

Derrick's physical body and astral body snapped together like strong magnets, slamming him back into the bed. His body jerked. Intermittent banging and dinging invaded his head. Then the familiar headache kicked in. Like an elastic band tight around his forehead, traveling down the base of his skull. His eyes jolted open. He stared for a long moment, disoriented, before slowly sitting up in bed. Bullington's podcast continued to play.

"... oh, yeah. Give them freedom then lock them up in prison cages for years. That's all I'm saying. Thanks for tuning in."

Once he got his bearings, Derrick grabbed his laptop from the nightstand and opened the lid. The brilliant screen illuminated his tense face as it booted up.

He opened a new email and typed 'task completed', encrypted the data, then tapped the 'send' button. It would only be a matter of seconds before he received confirmation that the payment had been transferred to his account at the Panama National Bank under the name, Miles McGrath. A million dollars. Not bad for less than two hours work including surveillance. A soft beep. Then a message popped up on the screen.

((0400TCHCLVGHEPUOFJJHPLJO7IAJKH))

With a couple of keystrokes, he ran the special decryption software he'd been given, and within seconds the garbled message became readable.

Fee transferred. Face-to-face requested

He shut down the laptop and wondered why his contact had requested a meeting in person. His face reflected on the black screen, yet his blue eyes shone.

About the Author

Kim Cresswell resides in Ontario, Canada and is the award-winning author of the action-packed WHITNEY STEEL series.

Her romantic thriller, *Reflection* (A Whitney Steel Novel - Book One) has won numerous awards: RomCon®'s 2014 Readers' Crown Finalist (Romantic Suspense), InD'tale Magazine 2014 Rone Award Finalist (Suspense/Thriller), UP Authors Fiction Challenge Winner, Silicon Valley's Romance Writers of America (RWA) "Gotcha!" Romantic Suspense Winner, and an Honorable Mention in Calgary's (RWA) The Writer's Voice Contest.

Kim recently signed a 3-book German translation deal with LUZIFER-Verlag for the first three books in the Whitney Steel series: *Reflection*, *Retribution,* and *Resurrect*. The popular series will be published in German beginning in 2018/2019.

The Assassin Chronicles TV series, based on Kim's upcoming 4-book paranormal/supernatural thriller series: *Deadly Shadow* (May 2018)*, Invisible Truth, Assassin's Prophecy*, and *Vision of Fire* is in development with Council Tree Productions.

www.kimcresswell.ca
www.facebook.com/KimCresswellBooks
http://twitter.com/kimcresswell

Also by Kim Cresswell

Whitney Steel Series
Reflection
Retribution
Resurrect

The Assassin Chronicles Series
Deadly Shadow

Raina Storm Series
Dawn of the Storm
Dawn of the Enemy

Single Title Novellas
Lethal Journey

True Crime Short Stories
Real Life Evil
Murder on Sunset Strip
Garden of Bones
Edge of Madness

'True Crime Anthologies Published by Grinning Man Press

Serial Killer Quarterly "21st Century Psychos"
Serial Killer Quarterly "Partners in Pain"
Serial Killer Quarterly "Unsolved in North America"
Serial Killer Quarterly "Cruel Britannia"
Serial Killer Quarterly "They Almost Got Away"
Serial Killer Quarterly "Lostmord: Murder in German"